THE
SPELLBOUND
HOTEL

THE SPELLBOUND HOTEL

TOM EGLINGTON

PICCADILLY PRESS • LONDON

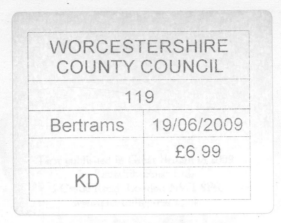

Mixed Sources
Product group from well-managed
forests and other controlled sources
www.fsc.org Cert no. TT-COC-002227
© 1996 Forest Stewardship Council

FSC

To my family,
for always supporting me,
and to Liz, Andy and Ruth,
for all their help along the way

CHAPTER ONE

WHAT ABOUT DAVE ?

To Bethany's eyes, there were many peculiar things in the village, but by far the most peculiar was the giant Stoames mansion that dominated the skyline and which she couldn't help thinking was growing larger day by day. It seemed no matter which street she turned down or which direction she faced, there was some part of the stately home staring back at her. Whether it was the rows of glinting windows, or the turrets and alcoves of its jagged roofing, or even the walls of lumpy masonry, the house was always there, always watchful. And since they had moved to Stagtree Knoll it felt as if it was there a little more every time she looked.

Stagtree Knoll wasn't like other villages. It was a place so strange that cats and dogs wandered about in a quiet daze, sharing worried looks with one another. Their owners were as unaware of this un-animal-like behaviour as they were of the encroaching mansion. All they seemed to be interested in was what new variety of sausage was available from the local butcher and what had happened the previous night on the soap opera, *What About Dave?*

The adults loved *What About Dave?* and would talk passionately about the latest plot development as they gathered in the long, eager queue outside the butcher's shop on the High Street. It was the only time Bethany saw the locals become animated. Every afternoon her mother sent her out to buy sausages for that evening's supper and she would have to endure the same debate as she waited in line. Today, she was trying her very hardest to ignore the people barging into her and talking directly over her head.

'No, Dave's childhood sweetheart isn't coming back,' a man nearest to her said loudly. 'I'm telling you, that boat has sailed.'

'But the fortune-teller said he could expect an old acquaintance to return with good news,' a woman in a headscarf replied knowingly. 'Who else could it be?'

A third voice added, 'It's his friend, Little Pete. You know, the one that disappeared eight episodes back after he discovered the map.'

'I thought that was Big Pete.'

'No. Big Pete found the map but Little Pete ran off with it, didn't he?'

'Never mind the Petes, what about Dave and this boat you mentioned?'

Bethany found herself involuntarily sighing and rolling her eyes. More voices joined in, arguing then agreeing then guessing what would happen in that night's episode, until the whole discussion became a meaningless rabble of noise. It was only when the villagers entered the shop that they finally settled down and concentrated on the important task of deciding which sausages they wanted. Even this would involve quiet muttering.

'Hmmm. Maybe I'll try the Leeky Glamorgan or . . . no, wait, that Jaunty Cumberland looks good today. Difficult, difficult.'

The sausages sat in neat pink piles behind the glass counter and the adults stared at them greedily, so much so that they barely gave the butcher a second look as he patiently and silently served them. He was a stout man dressed in a white uniform with a red striped apron and an old-fashioned straw hat that was always tipped forward at an angle so that his face remained hidden, and was perhaps why no one looked at his features very closely. Bethany, being smaller than everyone else, had a very clear view and could look at nothing else. It was why she disliked coming into the shop so much.

The butcher's face was nearly as white as his uniform and it was constantly fixed with a wide grin. His teeth were perfect, his hair – what she could see of it – was never out of place. His eyes, concealed under the wide brim of his hat, stared straight ahead and glittered with a strange light, making Bethany think of the glass eyes of dolls. She was sure she had never seen the butcher blink in all the times she had been here. It made the hairs on the back of her neck stand up.

'Come on, we don't have all day, young lady.' The man behind her shooed her forward impatiently and Bethany realised it was her turn to order. She stepped forward nervously.

'Um . . . Yes,' she said, momentarily distracted by the grinning face that hung above her. She pointed vaguely in the direction of the sausages and, in a high voice, said, 'Those, please. Half a dozen.'

The butcher's head nodded ever so slightly and he glided effortlessly behind the counter, picking out and wrapping six plump sausages. The usual thoughts rushed through Bethany's head. She wanted to ask what sort of things they used to make the sausages or why, if they were a butcher's, they didn't sell any other meat – or even discuss the weather to see how the butcher might react or if he could even speak. She was too frightened to say any of these things, though, as the blank eyes glimmered at her. The butcher passed her the package and pointed at the price on the cash register. Bethany thrust a five-pound note at him, fighting the urge to run off. Mercifully, as soon as she'd got the change, another customer barged forward to place their order and Bethany took the opportunity to scuttle away.

She didn't like going to the butcher's but her mother insisted it was a good way for her to meet some of the local people. Bethany didn't think that made a lot of sense. She had never seen any children her age there and all the adults ignored her. Anyway, she had tried her hardest to find friends to play with but Stagtree Knoll always seemed deserted. It was the middle of the summer holidays and yet no one was playing in the park, or exploring the woods that bordered one side of the village, or even causing trouble in the streets.

The one time Bethany had actually found children her age, they were standing in a garden deciding who would pretend to be the television and who would be the one watching it. As soon as she suggested going to the park their eyes glazed over and they went quiet. Without a word, they drifted back into their homes.

Today she walked up a couple of streets she had not been along before, hoping to meet someone. The first street was typically quiet, but halfway up the second she caught sight of a plump woman with rosy cheeks striding towards her. She had the look that a lot of the locals had. It was the sort of look that suggested they had left the house to do something very important but they couldn't quite remember what it was.

'Good afternoon,' Bethany said as she neared her.

The woman gave the usual bewildered response that she was used to.

'Well, yes,' she said unsurely. 'I suppose it might be.' She cheerfully posted a letter into the slot of an old litter bin before wandering off in the opposite direction, smiling idiotically.

Bethany sighed. There was something very wrong in Stagtree Knoll. It wasn't just the butcher or the sausages or *What About Dave?* It was the way that everyone behaved in the same confused, gormless manner. Shopkeepers gave away too much change, people left their homes for work still wearing their slippers, there was even a local policeman who regularly locked his keys in his police car. The whole village had lost its collective mind and it was driving Bethany crazy.

She picked the letter out of the bin, shaking free a piece of mouldy banana skin, and posted it in the letter box on the other side of the street. She wandered home, trying not to think about the Stoames mansion or the shadow it cast over their house.

As she stepped through the front door she could hear her mother shifting one of the chairs in the front room. She had pushed the sofa and an armchair up against one wall and was considering it with a puzzled frown. 'What do you think?' she asked before Bethany had closed the door. 'Does it look better this way?'

'Um, isn't it sort of like it was the last time you changed it?' she said, looking round the room. 'You know, when you moved it yesterday?'

If she heard her daughter, she pretended not to. Mrs Chase nodded her head. 'Yes, it is a bit roomier, isn't it? Although . . .' Doubt passed over her face. 'Maybe the armchair would be better by the window.'

'I was thinking,' Bethany said in a loud voice to get her mother's attention. 'Maybe today we could go for a walk together? You know, get out of the house for a bit. According to the local map there's a marsh out past the woods. It might be interesting.'

Her mother heaved the armchair towards her. 'That would be nice, dear,' she said.

Bethany looked at her disbelievingly. 'What? Really?'

'. . . But I've got to get on with this. *And* get supper ready.

You can go, though. Just make sure you're back by six.'

Bethany gave out a deep, exasperated sigh and dropped the packet of sausages on the table, deflated. 'It doesn't matter.'

Her mother looked up for the first time. 'Did you get the Herby Porkshire?' she asked, quickly picking up the packet and examining the contents.

Bethany walked off sulkily.

'Bethany?' Mrs Chase sounded momentarily concerned. 'Are you sure you're okay? I did ask you to get our usual.'

'I'm fine,' she said through gritted teeth. *But you're not*, she wanted to add.

Before coming to Stagtree Knoll, Bethany's mother would have been the one dragging her out on country walks or forcing her to appreciate some historical ruin. Now all she seemed to do was repeat the same jobs that she had done the first few days they had arrived here. Bethany didn't know what was wrong with her. She was as bad as the locals. She spent most of her days in a vague trance doing things that didn't really need doing and in the evenings sat down to yet another dinner of bangers and mash. And every night at exactly six-thirty, Mr and Mrs Chase settled into the sofa and watched the latest episode of *What About Dave?* It had been so different at first.

The day of the move had been exciting. Mr Chase had hired a large van which they had crammed full with all their possessions and the three of them had sat together on the wide front seat as they set off down the motorway for their new home. It was a hot, bright day and the roads were full of cramped family cars leaving the city for their summer holidays. Neither the traffic jams nor the sound of squabbling motorists could dampen their mood, though. The Chases sang along to the radio, told each other terrible jokes and played several of Bethany's made-up games.

'What's the name of the village again?' Bethany had asked when they ran out of things to do.

'I've said already,' her dad replied. 'It's called Stagtree Knoll.'

'Stagtree Knoll,' she repeated. 'It sounds old-fashioned. Does it mean anything?'

'I don't know. It's just a name, I think,' he said. 'Speaking of which . . .'

Mr Chase braked suddenly as they approached a large rusted signpost and he steered down a narrow country lane. Low branches scratched and thumped the roof of the van as they all bounced and rocked in their seats on the uneven road. They drove down increasingly smaller, bumpier roads and it seemed they were on the verge of being completely lost when they came to a clearing. All three of them turned expectantly to look at their new home at the same moment.

A rather drab, unremarkable village stood in front of them. There was an old church, a park and, further back, behind an estate of terraced houses, was the factory where Mr Chase would be working. It all had a neglected appearance to it, the gardens overgrown with weeds, the rows of houses run-down. By far the strangest landmark, though, was an old stately mansion that sat at one end of the High Street. It towered over everything else in the village, a huge, ominous construction that sat in its own private grounds. The peaked roofing jutted out at every angle as if the whole building was in the process of sprouting and it gave off a gloomy, imposing atmosphere.

None of them made a sound as they stared at it.

Eventually, Bethany's mother broke the silence. 'Paris. New York. Stagtree Knoll. You take us to all the best places.'

'Come on,' Bethany's father replied, trying to sound enthusiastic. 'It's exciting.'

Bethany kept quiet whilst they drove the few blocks to their new house. She knew she shouldn't act disappointed as it would only make her parents feel bad, so she tried her best to look pleasantly surprised at their new home, even though she thought it looked small and dull.

Mr Chase was first in the house, doing a quick inspection of all the rooms. They didn't waste any time in unpacking the van. They each took it in turns to carry a box and stack it in the hallway. Mr Chase made it his job to lug in the television set and find a place for it in their new lounge. 'Let's get our priorities straight, eh?' he said, winking.

As he began to fiddle with the reception, a picture appeared on the screen of an unconvincing hospital ward. He tried to change the channel but found only hissing static. 'If we can't get football, we're moving back,' he joked.

He might as well have been talking to the television as Bethany was peeking out of the windows at the dark silhouette of the Stoames mansion, counting its turrets, while her mother was busy carrying in the cardboard boxes and dumping them in the hallway.

Mr Chase chuckled to himself loudly to get some attention then said, 'This is *terrible*. Come and look at this. It must be some regional channel. Look.'

Bethany's mother huffed as she struggled with a bag of clothes. She dropped it at the door as loudly as she could. 'We need to get these things in before it gets dark.'

'I know, but you've got to see this. Really. It's terrible! Come and look.'

Bethany wandered over from the window. On the screen a woman was lying in a hospital bed covered from head to toe in bandages. She gasped melodramatically. A young doctor was taking her pulse and telling her that, yes, he was afraid it was terminal.

'You have a rare bone disorder that is currently untreatable. Spongiform skeletalitis. Put bluntly, Mrs Cutchley, your bones are turning to jelly.'

The bandaged woman sobbed loudly. 'But . . . but what about Dave?'

The doctor shook his head dolefully. 'Dave will have to soldier on without you.'

Bethany's father was laughing so hard that his belly heaved up and down. Her mother sat beside him on the floor and she grabbed Bethany and plonked her down between them as they giggled. The scenery wobbled. The microphone appeared in the top of the picture. The woman in the bed groaned theatrically and pretended to faint. It was so bad that the three of them let out a howl of laughter that rang throughout the entire house. Her mother's laughter turned into piggish squeals and her father's face went a bright red while Bethany was bounced around in the middle.

An angry thumping came from the wall as their neighbours banged for them to be quiet. They had turned up the volume on their own set to block out the racket and it was clear they were watching the same programme.

'Oh dear,' Mr Chase said, wiping his eyes. He tried to compose himself. 'Better not start off on the wrong foot, eh? Maybe we better get the rest of those things.' With a heavy sigh he switched off the TV, pulled himself up from the floor and carried on with the tasks of shifting and sorting their boxed belongings. It had been a tiring journey and they still had a lot to do.

By the next day it was becoming gradually more obvious how strange Stagtree Knoll was. The three of them went for an afternoon walk only to find the streets empty and the few people they did bump into looking very confused: a man being walked by his pet dog, a woman who had left her shopping in a newsagent's and an old lady who was standing impatiently by a tree as if it was a bus stop.

It didn't help matters later when Bethany answered the front door to a stout, beefy-looking man and his mousey wife. They looked at her blankly for a moment. 'Any parents?' the man asked bluntly.

Bethany fetched her mother and the couple smiled nervously at her.

'We're from next door,' the woman explained. She nudged her husband.

'Oh, yes.' He dropped a package into Mrs Chase's hands. 'A little something to welcome you to the village. And to say sorry for the banging.'

Bethany's mother undid the wrapping. A curious expression filled her face as she tried to force a smile of gratitude. 'Sausages! How . . . erm . . . how lovely. What a thoughtful gift.'

'They're gourmet, you know,' the woman said, smiling.

'Herby Porkshire,' her husband added.

'Yes, well, these really are . . . What a treat! Thank you very, very much.' Mrs Chase had to hurriedly shut the door as she had suddenly started giggling uncontrollably.

She was still trying to stop herself from giggling later on when she served the sausages for supper. Mr Chase cast a disapproving look at her. 'Come on now. You shouldn't laugh. It was a nice gesture.'

'But if we laugh loudly enough they might bang on the wall again and then give us some more sausages tomorrow,' Bethany said.

'Bethany, that's enough,' Mr Chase said, though he smirked.

It made her mother laugh even more. This in turn made Bethany giggle, but her father held up his hands, determined to stop a repeat of the previous night. 'Let's just try them before we make any harsh judgements, okay? It's only polite.'

Eventually Bethany and her mother contained themselves. They both watched as Mr Chase took the first bite of the sausages. He chewed. He frowned. He chewed again. A look of surprise crossed his face, mingled with a look of intense satisfaction. He took another, larger bite of the sausage and let out a gratifying, 'Mmmmm.'

At first, Bethany thought her father must be joking but then she noticed her mother was doing exactly the same thing. Mrs Chase tried a bite of the sausage and looked simultaneously amazed and confused at the same time as if she couldn't quite tell what it was she was tasting and had to try more. They both began to gobble their food, scoffing the sausages down in greedy mouthfuls, getting noisier and more frenzied.

Bethany looked down at her plate and frowned. It was only because she had stuffed herself with sweets in the afternoon that she didn't feel particularly hungry, but it stopped her long enough to notice the change that came over her parents. And that made her reluctant to even try the sausages.

Their eyes became glassy. Their mouths hung open slightly like they did when they were extremely tired. Even their voices took on a slow, distant quality. 'Now that,' Mr Chase said, lazily jabbing the air with his finger for emphasis, '*that* was a sausage.'

Mrs Chase nodded her head in full agreement. She sighed. 'I think I'm going to flop in front of the TV. I feel exhausted.'

'A good plan,' Mr Chase agreed.

Bethany had successfully moved the food around her plate without eating any of it. 'I'll save mine for later,' she said.

Both her parents seemed too tired to disagree. They

wandered through to the front room to watch television and Bethany could hear the same terrible soap opera with the same terrible actors. As she put the dishes in the sink she noticed a glowing out of the corner of her eye. She looked up through the window and saw the ghostly blue television light in every visible house flickering simultaneously. It made the village look like it was pulsating with a curious, hypnotic light. With the first stirrings of doubt, Bethany realised there was something strange going on, something very strange indeed.

That was five weeks ago now. Mr and Mrs Chase had fallen into the same habits as the other residents of Stagtree Knoll and Bethany didn't like it. She wasn't sure what was happening or why but she was determined to find out. She had spent the last week investigating the village in the hope of finding some clues and she had a funny feeling that tonight she was going to discover something important.

Idly, she peeked out of her window and found herself counting the turrets of the Stoames mansion as she had that first day. She kept counting them over and over again. It didn't make sense; no matter how many times she counted them, there were six extra turrets.

CHAPTER TWO

THE TOURISTS

'Mmmm, lovely,' Mr Chase said as Mrs Chase placed a full dinner plate in front of him. 'Bangers and mash.'

'Again,' Bethany added glumly.

Mrs Chase's smile faltered. 'Come on, Bethany. It's not like we have them all the time.'

'But we *do* have them all the time.'

Both her parents looked at her blankly.

'We're very lucky, you know. You wouldn't get this sort of thing in our old place,' her father said.

'That's true,' she sighed. She inspected the things on her plate with a mixture of boredom and suspicion.

It didn't matter if she told them that she had turned vegetarian or that she only wanted to eat fish or that she was tired of sausages. Each night the same meal appeared on her plate. It was, Bethany thought, as if they were stuck on repeat after the first time they had tried them and they didn't realise what they were doing.

Luckily, they were so busy guzzling their own food that they didn't notice their daughter carefully hiding hers in a napkin. Once she realised she couldn't talk her way out of mealtimes, Bethany had perfected the art of faking it. She cut up her sausages into tiny pieces and dropped them into a napkin laid out on her lap then mimed chewing them. She made sure to eat up all the mash and mushy peas. When her parents mmmmed with satisfaction she mmmed along with them.

Almost as soon as they slurped up the last of their food, Bethany leaped out of her chair and scooped up the plates. 'I'll tidy up,' she said.

Her parents made the usual series of satisfied sighs and groans without really acknowledging her. She carefully disposed of her napkin in the bin and started searching through the fridge for something normal to eat. 'I was thinking how we've not had a nice pie in a while,' she suggested. 'You know, chicken and mushroom or —'

When she turned back round, though, her parents were already wandering through towards the TV as if it was summoning them. Their faces had developed the slack-jawed, glassy-eyed expression Bethany knew all too well. An irritating jingle announced the start of *What About Dave?*

She hated the programme now. It always had the same stupid storyline which involved lots of people in a hospital shouting and crying and asking, 'What about Dave?'

Although Dave never actually appeared. Worse still, her parents were absorbed by it. They didn't find it funny or ridiculous any more but considered each catastrophic plot twist with genuine gasps of concern and they too wondered how this was going to affect Dave. It seemed while it was on, they were oblivious to the rest of the world, including their only child.

Bethany had tried watching it with them on a couple of occasions but it always made her feel drowsy, and she didn't like the way that once you started an episode you found yourself completely transfixed by it until the end. Then you wanted to watch more – although Bethany didn't watch more because she didn't want to end up like the locals. She made sure to stay away from the television whenever she heard the title music begin.

'Can I go out and play?' she asked.

'Hmmm?' Her mother shifted in her seat but couldn't draw her eyes away from the screen. She was chewing her lip. 'What's that? Yes, of course, dear. Yes, whatever you want. I mean . . .' She gasped at something on the telly and forgot what she was saying or to whom she was saying it.

Bethany quickly ran out of the door. The rows of houses glowed and flickered in unison, the same hollow TV noises echoed across the village. She skipped down the steps and along the narrow alley that led to the park, humming the tune to her favourite song.

For the last couple of weeks now Bethany had been wandering about Stagtree Knoll while everyone else watched the soap opera. At first, she had enjoyed having the entire village to herself as it meant she could do all sorts of things, like last Monday when she had swapped the plants between two gardens, or the Wednesday before when she constructed a circle out of small stones in front of the church to suggest paranormal forces were at work in the village. Then Bethany found out she wasn't the only one taking advantage of the empty streets.

Last Thursday she had been busy trying to see if she could remove a street sign and place it upside down when she had heard people walking around one of the streets up by the factory. She went to investigate but found the street empty by the time she got there. It made her uneasy and she wondered if it had anything to do with all the other strange things going on in Stagtree Knoll. The next night she had crept around the village cautiously, trying not to be seen. She went to spy on the same street but instead thought she saw some people walking into the woods. Again, she was too slow to catch them and by the time she got there, all she could find were several footprints in mud. Last night, though, she saw the gate of the Stoames mansion open at about the same time *What About Dave?* was starting and thought she glimpsed the butcher disappearing into the grounds as several strangers scuttled out.

Tonight, she had a plan. She ran up and down the gardens and collected all the ornamental gnomes she could find. She lined them up outside the window of the travel agent's as if they were browsing for holidays. If anyone walked down the High Street they would immediately spot them. It was on a direct route back to the Stoames mansion. All she needed to do was make some other suitable distractions on the other roads that led to the mansion gates and she would be able to get a look at any strangers from a safe distance.

Bethany positioned the last gnome by the bus stop when she heard voices over by the park. Even at this distance she could make out a clear, well-spoken accent that she had heard once in the local newsagent's.

Sir Jeremy Stoames spoke in a high, nasal voice that was instantly recognisable. He rarely appeared in the village but when he did everyone stopped to look at him. He was always dressed in a tweed suit and tweed hat. He had neat black hair and a pencil-thin moustache, and he walked with his head held high so that his large, extremely hairy nostrils were clearly visible to everyone. Bethany's dad thought he was strange because he insisted on being called Sir Stoames by everyone he met, even though Mr Chase reckoned he should be called Sir Jeremy and, if he was a proper Sir, he would know that. He also used a walking cane, even though there appeared to be nothing wrong with his legs.

'Yes, yes. Come along,' he was saying. 'It's just up here. Bear in mind we are in real time and there is only another ten minutes left of the tour, so please, be quick.'

Real time? Bethany thought. *What was he talking about?*

She watched the tweed hat moving confidently behind a tall hedgerow and several black hats bobbing after it like a duck and its ducklings. They were walking towards the playground at the far end of the park. She managed to sneak up to a low wall and peer over it to get a clearer look at the group as they came out into the open.

Three men and three women followed Sir Stoames across the grass. They were dressed in black suits and dresses, each wearing a formal black hat. From a distance Bethany could just make out the pale skin and impeccably neat hair that reminded her instantly of the butcher, not to mention the fixed smiles made up of perfectly white teeth. Even from this viewpoint she could see that their eyes glinted in the same way as the butcher's did and it made her crouch lower for fear of being spotted by them.

Sir Stoames led them to an old rusting roundabout, slide and climbing frame. A few of them took photos, which seemed a relatively normal thing for tourists to do, but most of them kept prodding things as if they were checking they were real. The group acted like they had never been outside before, never mind to a park. One of the women was fascinated by the long grass and kept brushing her fingers through it. Another had reached the roundabout and was closely inspecting it.

'So this, as you can see, is the park,' Sir Stoames said. 'In contrast to their living areas we've just visited, this is a place for physical recreation for both adults and children.'

Two of the men and one of the women were attempting to use the roundabout. Sir Stoames rocked back and forth on his heels, patiently checking his watch. 'Yes, yes, very good. Careful not to bang yourself. Don't damage the bodies. No. No, Mr Quinn, I don't think that will take your —' His voice suddenly rose in volume. 'Mr Quinn! You're a little large for that!'

One of the men was attempting to walk up the steps of the slide and the metal was crumpling under his weight. He was short and very fat and looked down unsurely at the damage his body was doing. Reluctantly, he shuffled away from the slide and made a disappointed wheezing noise.

Sir Stoames rapped his walking stick on the ground to get everyone's attention. 'Time to go back to the hotel. We only have five minutes.'

The tourists followed him as he strode towards the High Street. Bethany moved quickly to another hiding place behind a postbox so that she could watch the group from a closer vantage point. They approached the travel agent's with the garden gnomes waiting outside it and she felt a thrill of panic. But as Sir Stoames led the way, he pointed to some architectural feature of the mansion at the moment they passed them so that everyone missed Bethany's handiwork. She couldn't help feeling a little disappointed.

Mr Quinn straggled behind, waddling his short legs to keep up with the others. He stopped as the group moved on and it was as he was catching his breath that he noticed the gnomes at his feet. A strange noise erupted from his throat, a coughing, gargling, hiccupping noise. He slapped his hands over his mouth to silence himself then very carefully, very purposefully, clicked his fingers at the gnomes.

At that moment Bethany caught a glimpse of something extremely peculiar and wonderful. The garden gnomes shook with movement. They rattled on the ground and began to hop about as if someone was jerking them upwards on strings. Mr Quinn pointed his finger. One by one, the gnomes hopped down the street in the direction he'd pointed and lined up outside the butcher's doorway, making them look like exceedingly small villagers waiting to buy sausages. Mr Quinn's grin widened and he rushed off after the other tourists.

For a full minute Bethany couldn't move and wasn't sure if what she had just witnessed was a trick or actual magic. Her first reaction was to laugh. It was quickly followed by an urge to find out what these strange people were up to. *If they could do magic, what else could they do? And what did Sir Stoames mean by hotel?* Bethany had never seen any guests enter the mansion before and she was sure she had never heard any of the locals mention it being a hotel.

Without another thought, she ran after the group. They had already reached the long gravel driveway that curved up to the gates of the mansion. She sprinted over to the ornamental trees that bordered the driveway and hid behind one. Sir Stoames prattled on in a dull monologue about the history of the village. It was joined by the sounds of Mr Quinn's strained breathing and the crunching of gravel underfoot. The noise made it a lot easier for Bethany to get up close, undetected. She dared herself to sneak all the way up to the tree nearest the gate and, in rapid bursts, dashed from one tree to the next until she was only a few feet away from the tourists. She heard one of them turn in her direction and make a puzzled noise.

The whole group turned and Bethany felt her heart leap out of her chest. How was she going to explain herself? There was a long, uncomfortable silence. The sort that comes before any kind of trouble. She tried to think of a plausible excuse.

Sir Stoames snorted. 'Oh, that. Awfully impressive, eh? That's the broadcast finishing. We use it in conjunction with an edible soporific. It keeps the locals in an *occupied* state. Just a little something Jickonuss . . . Juckofish . . . Jappo – *our generous host* arranged so that your tour is more enjoyable. '

Bethany sighed with relief.

'After all, we don't want you mixing with the riff-raff, do we?' Sir Stoames quipped.

The group chuckled politely, all except Mr Quinn who looked around at the others in a slightly surprised way. Something about Sir Stoames and the other tourists must have amused him because his smile broadened and his body wobbled and quivered. The gurgling, hiccupping noise started again, but this time sounded like an engine revving. He took a single, deep breath inwards that shook the bushes and whipped hats off heads. The others edged away from him and Sir Stoames suddenly looked panic-stricken. He waved his cane in the air.

'NO!' he shouted. 'No laughing, Mr Quinn. Don't you do it. Not out here. I'm warning you! You know what'll happen. Don't you dare!'

Mr Quinn made the pained noises of someone trying to hold in a laugh. It whistled through the gaps of his teeth. His chest heaved with the effort of holding it in. It looked for a moment as if he might explode with the sheer effort of containing it. His eyes rolled in their sockets this way and that, and he briefly glimpsed Bethany hiding behind the bush. She held up a single finger to her mouth in a silent *shoosh*, hoping he could keep a secret. The shock must have been enough to distract Mr Quinn. He managed to calm himself enough to let out a deep, shuddering breath.

Sir Stoames adjusted his tilted hat and removed a key from his pocket. It was very old and large and made the workings of the lock creak as it turned. The tourists disappeared through the open gate after him. Mr Quinn was last and he waddled in. He paused to look back at Bethany. He raised a single finger to his mouth, winked conspiratorially then nodded in the direction of the ground.

Bethany glanced down and found that a hat had landed a few feet from her. She wondered if Mr Quinn had moved it there in the way he had moved the gnomes. Cautiously, she picked it up. She wanted to know who these strangers were and why they looked like the butcher and how, most importantly, they were involved with the broadcast of a programme that had turned her parents into mindless addicts. In a rush of nervous excitement, she flung the hat on her head and ran after the group of strangers, looking like an extremely short and late addition to the group.

Luckily, one of the tourists was questioning Sir Stoames about the significance of the coat of arms on the front of the gate, so that no one noticed Bethany joining them. They all stared at the image of an antlered stag's head merged with the branches of an oak tree and a golden arrow glowing mysteriously at the centre.

'Oh, that's nothing, really. An old family coat of arms,'

Stoames said dismissively. 'Well, we have timed things well. I hope you've all enjoyed your tour.'

With these words, he pulled the huge, thick gate closed behind them. The group shuffled forward through the darkness and into the grounds of the mansion. As she was much lower than everyone else and partially hidden by Mr Quinn's massive frame, Bethany managed to go unnoticed. She could hear him spluttering, as if he was holding back another fit of laughter. It was just as well because Bethany couldn't help a loud, conspicuous gasp escaping from her mouth.

The spacious gardens surrounding them were full of stone statues that were positioned at regular intervals. Gigantic, ferocious-looking dogs glared down at them from stone plinths. The statues were incredibly realistic and the animals had been carved in a variety of poses. Some were sitting obediently, some had heads cocked as if they were sniffing the air for scents, others were on all fours waiting to pounce, and all of them were snarling. If that wasn't bad enough, they stood almost fifteen feet high, dwarfing the group of tourists.

Bethany felt nervous. *Maybe this is a mistake*, she thought. *Maybe it's best to go back now.*

The group had made it halfway up the path and she peered backwards at the closed gate and tried to remember if Sir Stoames had locked it. She began to purposefully loiter at the back so that she could make a run for it, but she had the eerie feeling that the stone dogs were watching her. She looked from one stone head to the next and each set of unblinking eyes seemed to be fixed on her. There were also two dogs standing guard by the gate that she hadn't seen when she came in. She must have been mistaken, though. Statues couldn't move or look at you.

Nerves gave way to outright panic and Bethany quickly caught up with the group.

'And remember,' Stoames was saying to the tourists, 'tours into the physical realm are just one of the many wonderful activities you can experience during your time at the hotel.'

She didn't understand what he meant by that but she was beginning to think it wasn't good. With each step closer to the mansion she was feeling more unwell. Not just nervous but a sick sensation, as if she were in a lift going down very fast. She looked back once more, deciding that she needed to make it home even if it meant running past the staring statues. When she turned to leave, though, she noticed that the stone dogs had definitely changed position. They were facing her and several had miraculously moved on to the path to block the way out.

'Oh, no . . .' Bethany uttered aloud, unable to believe what she was seeing. She felt a jolt of terror. *How had they done that? It wasn't possible.*

Mr Quinn quickly covered up the noise by coughing loudly so Bethany would not attract Sir Stoames's attention.

Bethany tried to tell herself not to panic as she started panicking. Her stomach tightened and she could feel her breathing coming in short, quick gasps. Her eyes darted around. In front of her was the group of freakish tourists, behind her were the savage statues. This was bad. What had she been thinking?

A quick, terrified peek backwards revealed that the dogs had moved another ten feet forward. They were caught in a leaping pose, their jaws open, displaying rows of jagged teeth. Somehow they had managed to completely obscure the path and were merging together like an advancing pack. No one else seemed to have registered what was going on. Sir Stoames had reached the arched entrance to the mansion and calmly searched his pockets for the correct key.

Bethany's head swayed and she couldn't help groaning. The sick feeling became more intense as her stomach flipped over. She felt she was about to faint.

Mr Quinn's chubby face swivelled round to inspect her. His breathing groaned questioningly like the gurgling sound of a bagpipe. It was difficult to tell if his expression showed shock, concern or amusement at Bethany's condition, but he blinked at her three times, very precisely, and tapped her at the back of her neck. She felt something pass through her in a wave and the sickly feeling dissolved away.

When she looked up to him for an explanation, Mr Quinn's attention had already shifted to the door. The group moved in single file through the entrance. Bethany dared one last backwards glance. The dogs had merged into a ravenous pile and formed an impenetrable wall of stone. There was no way out now. She had to join the others in the mansion.

Bethany stepped through the doorway.

CHAPTER THREE

In the Wrong Place

At first, things looked reassuringly normal inside the Stoames mansion. There was a long gothic hallway with a large wooden booth at the nearest end. A brass sign above it read *Cloakroom.* Beside it hung two large clocks set at different times like the clocks at airports. The clock nearest to her told the correct time and had a label underneath it that read, *Physical Realm.* The clock on the left, however, had a label underneath it that read, *Spirit Realm.* This clock only had one hand and, instead of numbers, there were lots of descriptions written around its edge: *Good, Funny, Bad, Fine.* The hand currently pointed to *Strange.*

Strange time, Bethany thought. It was at least accurate. She couldn't think of a time when things had been stranger for her. The sick feeling had passed but the outright terror hadn't gone away. She couldn't help checking the closed door behind her and wondering whether the stone dogs were obediently waiting outside it. What was she going to do? She couldn't just pretend she had accidentally wandered in there.

She was distracted by a sound ahead. The guests were lined up in front of the wooden booth. The old woman at the head of the queue fiddled with a zip between her shoulder blades but it wasn't just the zip to her clothing. As she pulled it down her head dropped forwards. Next, her entire arm flopped loose, then a leg, then the next arm. Bethany strained her neck and could now see that she had unzipped her spine and the opening revealed a patch of glowing light. The human body fell forwards, lifeless, as a brightly coloured shape pulled itself free from the opening. What looked like a majestic bird with beautiful plumage emerged. It was twice as tall as Bethany and made up from a brilliant, dazzling light that gave off glints of intense colours. It ruffled its red and yellow feathers and flitted away up the corridor, leaving faint traces of itself in the air behind it that glittered for several moments.

Bethany had never seen anything like it in her entire life. She was dumbstruck. She felt simultaneously amazed at the beauty of the creature and completely shocked at seeing something so unreal. *This can't be happening*, she thought. *What is going on here?*

The next tourist in line stepped out of its body as if stepping out of a costume. A grey, spectral figure pulled itself free. Like the bird it was made up from light, although dimmer and with the dense consistency of mist.

The strange being stretched as if it had just endured a long, cramped car journey and its gloomy face looked down at the human outfit it had removed itself from. It shook its head dolefully and drifted off. Something Bethany couldn't quite see moved across the floor and dragged the lifeless body to the cloakroom.

Bethany could barely breathe. *What was this place?*

The third creature was a pompous, walrus-like being that wore important robes and lavish jewellery. He clearly found the act of undressing himself distasteful as his foot became tangled in his human outfit. He grumbled at the leg and what seemed to be his shadow immediately separated itself from him and moved across the floor to help. It tugged at the human body, which came free, much to the satisfaction of the walrus creature, and his shadow pulled it across the floor to the cloakroom attendant.

'Next!' cried the attendant, as he hung the body against the wall inside the booth. This man had all the normal features of someone who might work as a desk clerk. He had a long face with wide, nervous eyes. He had a mop of receding hair that had curled up in tight, worried coils. He even wore wire glasses that kept sliding down his nose as he inspected his registration book. But all of these things were made up from a vague, bluish light, making him appear as though he was fading away. The other things looked fantastical and not entirely human, but this man was unmistakably a ghost.

It was too much. Bethany turned to the door and frantically jiggled the handle. She had to get out of there, even if that meant facing the stone guard dogs. She tried with all her strength to budge the door but it held fast. She turned expectantly to Mr Quinn with the sudden hope that he could help her in some way or at least protect her from the others. He was partly to blame for this mess.

Bethany went to grab Mr Quinn's arm but he was next in line and he stepped out of her reach. She watched as the human head slumped forwards and the real Mr Quinn pulled himself free. A humanoid figure appeared and immediately began to shrink in size until he was no bigger than Bethany's hand. He had an oval body made from the same gauzy light as the others, with spindly arms and legs that looked like they could barely support him. His face continued from his shoulders as if he had no neck and it boasted an impossibly wide grin that stretched from one lumpy ear to the other. His eyes glinted with mischief beneath a quiff of pink hair that topped his head in a neat squiggle. He leaped up into the air, pirouetted gracefully, saluted Bethany, and disappeared with an audible pop.

'Next!' cried the cloakroom attendant. Bethany moved forward as a shadow whisked away Mr Quinn's discarded human body. She was all that was left of the line. She gulped and stood in front of the booth, the top of her head level with the desk. Maybe she could create a diversion and escape, she thought. The ghost attendant clicked his fingers irritably. 'Body, please.'

'Um,' said Bethany. Panicking, she reached her hands behind her head and pretended to be trying to undo a zip while she tried to think of some way to get out of this mess. Her eyes searched for an escape route but there was only the

31

single corridor ahead of her. She made a motion with her hands that suggested the zip was stuck. This seemed a good decoy until her fingertips, much to her surprise, discovered that there was a zip at the top of her spine.

'Well?' said the ghost attendant impatiently. He was still scanning the old dusty book in front of him.

'Um,' said Bethany again, her voice very high and nervous. Her mind reeled. *No, no, no . . . This is bad. This is worse than bad. This is a type of bad that hasn't been invented yet.*

She wanted to run. She wanted to be back home. As the thoughts raced round her head, she momentarily wondered what would happen if she stepped out of her skin. Would she look like a muscle and bone version of herself or would she resemble some strange creature like the others? She felt strangely excited at the idea.

The ghost attendant sighed heavily. 'I'm afriad I really must insist . . .'

Bethany closed her eyes, inhaled deeply, and very slowly, very carefully pulled the zip down. She could feel her spine undoing itself. She checked the opening. No blood. She tested it with her fingers. No soft gooey bits. Instead, there was a warm, tingling patch. With a rush of fear and excitement she pulled it down as far as it would go. There was a strange sensation of being sucked through the tingling patch on her back and feeling something heavy drop away as she stepped backwards. Her body sunk to the floor. When she opened her eyes and looked at herself she was still there but she was now like a ghost. She was as transparent as the cloakroom attendant, although she didn't have the faded blue glow. Instead, she was a more colourful version of the body at her feet. The ghost skin was a bright pink. The ghost jeans were a vivid blue. Her red trainers shone as brightly as red traffic lights. It was like looking at a rainbow close-up.

'Whoa!' She stretched her transparent arms in front of herself so that she could see the walls through her hands.

Bethany's shadow stirred beneath her. She didn't know which was more disturbing, seeing it move by itself or watching it dutifully tug her body to the cloakroom attendant. The ghost placed a satisfying tick in his book. He used a chain to pull Bethany's body up against the wall and hang it from a large metal peg. A note of concern entered his voice as he turned back to his column of numbers, though.

'Number seven?' he said, checking his figures. 'How strange, I thought only six went —'

The cloakroom attendant never finished his sentence as he peered at Bethany. An expression of horror came over his face and his cheeks filled with colour, making him look strangely ill.

Bethany was too busy looking at the cloakroom. She had just noticed the body hanging from the first peg. 'Hey, that's the butcher,' she said loudly. Beside it was Sir Stoames's body, now hanging limp and lifeless. 'And that's —'

The cloakroom attendant stammered, 'S-Sir Stoames?'

Sir Stoames was standing further up the hallway talking to a tall cat as casually as if he were discussing the weather with a neighbour. He had somehow transformed into a ghostly version of himself, although instead of the pale blue of the cloakroom attendant he had an austere silvery-blue glow.

Bethany's attention shifted from the hanging bodies to the quaking cloakroom attendant. Everything seemed to be the wrong way round. Surely, she should be afraid of him and not vice versa. She leaned forward. 'Sorry, I didn't mean to scare you. Are you okay? It's just, you look like you've seen a —'

The man jumped backwards in terror. 'Sir Stoames!' he yelped.

Sir Stoames turned on his heels. 'What is it, Graceson? I'm frightfully busy.'

The attendant pointed a shaking finger at Bethany. Sir Stoames's jovial expression dropped instantly. 'Oh, my goodness me. You're . . . you're not one of the guests!'

Bethany opened her mouth to clear up the misunderstanding. She was sure there was some way she could explain everything. Unfortunately, that was the moment she noticed her shadow hurrying away from her. It skittered up the long hallway, joining all the other shadows as they rushed towards the far end. Before she could say anything to Sir Stoames it had disappeared halfway up the corridor.

Stepping out of her body was one thing but Bethany didn't want to lose her shadow as well. She had never given it much thought before, but now it was disappearing she had a sudden and desperate urge to get it back. She ran after it, hurtling away from the cloakroom attendant whose face was returning to its natural pale-blue colour. She shot past Sir Stoames and the cat, both of them gasping indignantly at her. Without a body to anchor it, her shadow moved faster than it ever had before, looking more like the speeding shadow a bird might cast as it flew high overhead. It had covered the length of the hallway in seconds and it quickly disappeared round a corner.

'Wait! Come back here!' Bethany shouted after her shadow.

'Wait! Come back here!' Sir Stoames shouted after Bethany.

'Wait!' the cloakroom attendant called feebly. 'Oh . . . never mind.'

Bethany sprinted to the end of the hallway and followed her shadow through a doorway. What she saw made her stop dead in her tracks.

She found herself standing in a large hotel foyer. At first glance it looked like the plush foyer of any grand hotel. It had red carpets leading to a busy reception area, there were plump leather armchairs dotted about in comfortable alcoves, and wide spiral staircases leading off to the rooms. In fact, it might have all seemed normal if it wasn't for the guests and the staff.

The guests were every bit as strange as the entities she had seen in the cloakroom. There were vaguely human ones, vaguely animal ones and some she had no idea about at all, each of them made from the same luminous substance. Directly across from her was a white fox entertaining a pig in a ballroom dress and a gigantic rat sipping a glass of champagne. They were staring at a large potato-like creature filling one of the many chairs, white shoots sprouting from his head towards a nearby lamp.

The human shapes were standing by an aquarium in the centre of the lobby. There was a beautiful woman who seemed to be made entirely out of water standing beside a man made entirely out of leaves. Two young children floated by their shoulders, looking like exceedingly plump babies with wings. They were all pointing at the brightly coloured fish in the tank which, much to Bethany's amazement, weren't fish at all but tiny mermaids and mermen. They were riding on seahorses and seemed to be involved in a game of waterpolo. The human-shaped group was cheering them on.

This scene was disrupted as another creature passed by. It seemed to be mostly invisible as the only indication it was there was the brief, fading traces of itself when it moved through the air, giving tantalising glimpses of a fantastic many-armed, many-headed being.

In comparison, the staff looked relatively normal. A dozen ghosts, dressed in the same grey uniform with the single letter *J* embroidered on their jackets in gold, were handing out keys at the reception desk, answering enquiries and giving directions. The rest of the staff consisted of the guests' shadows, which were darting across the floor, pulling at the shadows of suitcases and bags. These in turn pulled the objects themselves, making the baggage look like it was directing itself across the foyer. Occasionally, a shadow would get snagged on its owner and have to wrench itself free.

Above them all was a huge sign written in gold.

J's Hotel for Ghosts, Spirits and Non-material Beings.

The letter *J* split apart in golden spirals that spread on to the wallpaper to make up an elaborate, curlicue design. It gave the entire foyer a dazzling, dizzying appearance.

Bethany was so amazed by all this that she almost forgot about her own shadow. It was only when Sir Stoames's hand landed on her shoulder that she remembered what she was supposed to be doing.

'Explain yourself immediately, young lady,' he said in an authoritative tone. The cloakroom attendant came huffing and puffing behind him, his glasses slipping down his nose.

She glimpsed her shadow squirming amongst the throng of legs, immediately recognisable as it was the only child's shadow among all the other strangely shaped shadows. She threw herself after it, breaking free of Stoames's grip and plunging into the crowd of unusual guests. She barged past furry legs, slimy legs, feathered legs, tentacled legs. Gasps of shock followed her progress as spirits leaped out of her way. Sir Stoames followed, apologising profusely.

'No, no. Nothing to worry about. Just a little, um, practical joke. Please carry on.'

Her shadow slipped beneath a doorway with a large *Staff Only* sign on it. She pushed through the swing doors and found herself at the top of a wide staircase. The shadow staff trickled down the steps in a dark current of silhouettes. The baggage they had been pulling came tumbling and crashing down after them.

Rat-a-tat-TAT.

By the time they reached the bottom, most of the suitcases had smashed open and spilled their contents everywhere. The shadows were eagerly swarming around the scattered belongings. Two ghosts were re-packing the suitcases – clearly the shadows could only influence things connected with the floor. The ghosts moved quickly, trying desperately to keep up with the backlog of suitcases, filling them with whatever came to hand. Beyond them was a wide corridor lined with doors where the re-packed bags were being dragged away by more shadows, presumably to be delivered to the guests' rooms.

Bethany managed to keep her eyes on her own shadow as it crept down the stairs and joined the others in a tug of war over the possessions.

'Stop that now,' she commanded, unsure of how she should address it. 'That's not yours to play with.'

Her shadow hesitated.

Rat-a-tat-TAT.

Another suitcase came crashing down the stairs. She jumped out of the way. Her shadow scampered over the spilt belongings and pulled a toothbrush that was as large as a hairbrush towards the feet of one of the overworked ghosts. It was hastily thrown into a pink suitcase with an assortment of random objects.

'I saw that! You did that on purpose.' She felt like she was telling off a particularly badly behaved pet.

It turned its head as if it was looking up at her.

'Come back here. You're my shadow and I don't want you playing with this lot. We're going home.'

All the other shadows paused to face her direction. She felt a little uncomfortable. There was another *rat-a-tat-tat* sound and she dodged out of the way, only to find Sir

Stoames's hand landing on her shoulder again.

'I don't know who you are or what you think you are doing but YOU ARE IN THE WRONG PLACE!'

Bethany squirmed to try and break free and make another run for it but Sir Stoames tightened his grip and muttered, 'Mudgo tanglefinger'.

The fingers gripping her shoulder began to grow and curl in long squiggly columns, like toothpaste squeezed from a tube. As they extended, they wrapped round her ghost neck and ghost arms.

'Get off, get off,' she shouted, trying to peel the fingers away but soon found her hands trapped in the knotted tangle of fingers.

Sir Stoames raised his arm so that Bethany dangled above the ground. She immediately tried to kick him but found her legs wouldn't reach.

'Let go let go let go let go!'

'You are in the wrong place,' he said again.

The cloakroom attendant fidgeted nervously at Sir Stoames's side. 'Do you have to hold her so tightly? She looks upset.'

'I know exactly what I'm doing thank you, Graceson.'

And then all the panic and fear that had been building in Bethany from the moment she had stepped through the gate finally broke free in a long, loud scream.

The shadows stopped moving. The ghosts stopped packing the bags. There were even several guests peering through the doorway at the top of the stairs.

The force of the scream turned Bethany's face red. The

redness spread down her neck and along her arms. Sir Stoames's expression changed from a confident grin to a nervous frown. He was suddenly at the centre of attention, with the ghosts looking at him disapprovingly, and more guests gathering around the doorway at the top of the stairs.

Then the screaming turned into crying.

Sir Stoames lowered his arm. He cleared his throat. His cheeks were blushing darker blue. 'Now, now. There's no need for all this noise, young lady.'

Bethany paused just long enough to look at the tangled fingers then resumed crying.

'Umm. Right. Let's all just . . . calm down.' His eyes roamed around the room. Ghosts frowned, the shadows folded their arms, the guests scowled.

He muttered something under his breath and the fingers retracted back into his hand. He tried to laugh a good-natured laugh. Gritting his teeth, he said, 'Just stop making that noise . . . please.'

Bethany's sobbing slowed down to blubbering which turned into sniffling. She surveyed the room with a mixture of fear and fascination. The cloakroom attendant wrung his hands with worry.

Finally, a thought occurred to her that made her forget all about being stuck in a hotel full of ghosts and spirits. She looked up at Sir Stoames. 'Can you show me how to make my fingers do that?'

CHAPTER FOUR

QUESTION TIME

Bethany was full of questions as Sir Stoames walked her to his office. 'Are all those funny creatures spirits? Why can my shadow move on its own? Am I a ghost now? Only I thought ghosts could move through walls and these seem as solid as . . . well, walls. Is it that these are ghost walls, and if I was still in my body then I could walk through them like a ghost could walk through normal walls but because I'm a ghost I can't?'

Sir Stoames groaned as he led Bethany down a series of identical white corridors. His cane tapped a steady tempo on the floor. The walls were decorated in an intricate pattern of gold threads and each door they passed was a bright, glossy red. Bethany looked at them but could see no numbers.

Graceson, the cloakroom attendant, followed. He was trying to organise a pile of papers that he kept dropping, picking up, shuffling, then dropping again. 'Dear-oh-dear. This is all highly irregular. There's nothing in the rulebook about one of the living entering the hotel.'

'How did she get out of her body? That's what I would like to know, Graceson,' Sir Stoames said. He walked very quickly and both Bethany and Graceson struggled to keep up. They came to the end of one corridor and turned left, then came to the end of the next corridor and turned left again. The same line of blank doors passed by.

'I don't know,' replied Graceson. 'Her body had a spinal transmigration patch just like all the others.'

'That's impossible. You don't just suddenly grow a trans-migration patch. Look at her, Graceson. She's full of colours, she's a living human. She shouldn't have even been able to make it through the grounds.'

Bethany thought of the sick feeling she'd experienced as she had approached the mansion and the mysterious zip that appeared on her neck. A mysterious zip that had appeared at exactly the place Mr Quinn had tapped her to stop her feeling unwell. Her mind flashed with a sudden realisation. 'Oh!' she said very loudly.

'Oh, indeed,' Sir Stoames growled then turned to his assistant. 'I need not tell you how big a slip up this is.'

The ghost attendant flinched nervously. 'What are we going to do? The defences are up until tomorrow. If Jappofuss . . . Jickomutt . . . Juttofi— Oh! If *he* finds out we'll be in terrible trouble.'

Sir Stoames stopped in his tracks. He was grinding his teeth and his nostrils flared, making the hairs inside quiver with anger. 'No. *You* will be in terrible trouble, because I'll make sure he knows it's *your* blunder, Graceson. So you better make sure Jaggo— *he* doesn't find out!'

Bethany tugged Sir Stoames's elbow. 'Who is that you keep talking about? That Jaddomiss . . . Jottafitt . . . Jabbo—' She felt as if she was having a sneezing fit.

A hand clapped over her mouth before she could make any more attempts at saying it, followed by a second hand, then a third and a fourth. Both Graceson and Sir Stoames kept their hands clasped tightly over her mouth. She considered screaming again but noticed their faces were racked with worry. Their eyes darted about the corridor. Sure enough, something very strange was happening to the walls. A ripple of movement passed through the golden threads of the wallpaper. They squirmed and twisted and seemed to come alive. Several strands peeled away from the wall and probed the air like antennae.

Neither of the men moved or dared make a sound until the golden threads, unable to detect anything unusual, returned to their patterned arrangement on the wall. They relaxed with a palpable sense of relief. Sir Stoames immediately picked up his cane and waggled it at Graceson. In a very quiet, stern tone, he said, 'He can sense something isn't right, you know.'

'I just tried to say what you said,' Bethany explained.

'Yes, but we are familiar to . . . him. You, on the other hand, are a stranger here. A strange stranger: You're one of the living. The hotel doesn't like that. *He* doesn't like that.' He strode off up the corridor. 'Let's get to my office and I will explain a few rules.'

Bethany had to jog to keep up with him. 'It doesn't seem to me as though there are any rules here.'

Graceson flapped his sheaf of papers at her as if the huge messy bundle was the entire rulebook. He was struggling to put it back into some sort of order.

'There are rules,' said Sir Stoames. 'Just not the rules you are used to. But then you've broken the rules you are used to.'

'I didn't break any rules,' protested Bethany.

'So you normally jump out of your own body, do you?'

She couldn't think of a good answer to that so she deflected it with a question. 'Why do we keep walking in circles?'

'What do you mean?' said Sir Stoames, as he turned left at the end of another corridor. He must have done this over a dozen times now.

'We're always turning left. That means we're just going in circles.'

'Squares, actually,' Graceson corrected.

Sir Stoames shrugged as they reached the end of the corridor and turned left. There, ahead of them, was a much shorter corridor with a green door at the end of it.

'That's not possible,' Bethany said.

Sir Stoames beamed. 'As I said, there are different rules here.'

He whistled a short, three-note tune and the door swung open. He ushered Bethany inside and left Graceson to close the door behind them.

The office was not what could be considered a normal

office. In fact, it was so full of plants that it was hard to see any office at all. Bethany felt more like she was standing in the centre of a very dense, very pleasant forest. There were large leafy plants, giant ferns, sprouting nettles and a ring of tall, gnarly trees that seemed to make up the edges of the room.

Sir Stoames took a seat behind his desk, which was the remains of a wide tree trunk cut off at its base. Thin, crooked branches grew out of its sides. A clock hung from the tree behind him and Bethany noticed that its arrow pointed to *Question* time.

Graceson busied himself with filing away his papers. This consisted of climbing up and down the surrounding trees and opening drawers concealed by their bark. There had to be over a hundred drawers winding up each trunk and he moved quickly and purposefully, retrieving and depositing bundles of paper with the skill of an acrobat jumping from one branch to another.

'Please, take a seat,' Sir Stoames said.

Bethany looked around at the plants, unsure of what she was supposed to sit on.

'There, over there,' cried Graceson from a high-up branch.

She followed the pointing finger. Four saplings had grown out of the floor and knitted together to form a chair. She carefully sat in it, trying not to damage any of the fresh green shoots.

Sir Stoames rummaged through his desk. He opened drawers and slammed them shut again immediately, tutting and muttering. Small drawers opened out of bigger drawers that slid out of larger compartments. Whatever he was looking for wasn't there and his search became more frantic. He hitched up hatches, slid back slots, parted partitions. By the time he'd finished, his desk was twice its size with empty drawers telescoping out at every angle.

'No, no, no. I can't find it anywhere,' he sighed loudly in exasperation.

From the branches above him Graceson dropped a single sheet of paper that glided down like a falling leaf and landed perfectly on the desk.

'Ah, there it is. Right. Good.' He sat up straight in his chair, loosened his collar and examined the paper with a quizzical frown. He pulled a pencil from his top pocket and harrumphed.

'Name?'

Bethany crossed her legs. 'Bethany Chase.'

Sir Stoames quietly repeated it as he wrote it down.

'Age?'

'Twelve.' She looked at her shoes. She had answered questions like these before and they were always very boring. Some things were at least the same in the spirit realm. She noticed with a little interest that her chair had grown a few inches higher off the ground.

'Address?'

'Fifteen Stonebridge Road, Stagtree Knoll.'

'Yes, that's good.' Sir Stoames murmured and muttered as his pencil scribbled across the page. He paused for a moment, considered something, then underlined the address several times.

Bethany could hear Graceson rustling branches somewhere

above her. He sounded extremely high up.

'Profession?'

'Um . . . I don't have a profession.'

'Unemployed, eh?' Stoames tutted and shook his head. He sounded very disappointed.

'I am only twelve,' said Bethany. She looked back down at her shoes and saw that they were dangling a short way off the ground. The chair became a little more comfortable as it grew a thick covering of leaves.

'What order of being are you?' he asked. 'Ghost, spirit or other?'

This was a trickier question. Bethany examined herself uncertainly. 'I don't know. I suppose I look a bit like a ghost but . . . what's the difference between a ghost and a spirit?'

Stoames spluttered incredulously. 'What's the difference between a ghost and a spirit? Dear me, child!' He snorted and shook his head. 'You really have a lot to learn, don't you?'

'Well, I don't know,' Bethany said defensively. She was beginning to get annoyed by his attitude.

Sir Stoames sighed. His chair was also growing in height and his knees were level with the top of his desk but he didn't appear to be bothered about it. 'A ghost is the *imprint* of an individual person or creature. They tend not to have any of the magical attributes of spirits and fade after only a few hundred years. That's why you never see ghosts of cavemen.'

Bethany, although listening, couldn't help nervously peering over the edge of her seat as the saplings made crackling noises with their accelerated growth. 'And spirits?'

47

'Spirits are supernatural beings made from pure *essence*. They are the essence of the things they represent. There are dog spirits that represent the particular essence of dogs, there are tree spirits that represent the inherent nature of trees, there are river spirits that embody the essence of rivers. All spirits are powerful and generate the mysterious energy that is vital to all life. They are, on the whole, superior to ghosts. However, there are exceptions to these rules. I, for example, have a much higher status than your average ghost and higher than some spirits.'

Bethany ignored his smug tone and thought of the strange selection of beings she saw in the hotel foyer. The spirits had all glowed brightly as if they were generating their own light, the ghosts were faint and drab in comparison. 'So why do some of them look human and some just look . . . weird?'

'Well, it really depends on how much they like the human form. Most spirits can change their appearance. Some like looking human and some don't. And then there are all sorts of spirits that govern human nature.' The overhanging branches of the trees were only a few inches from the top of Sir Stoames's head. 'But maybe the question you should be asking is why do humans look so like spirits? After all, spirits have existed longer.'

Bethany made a puzzled noise.

He returned to his sheet of paper. 'Anyway, I think in your case we'll put down *Other*. You're certainly not a spirit and the ghost section doesn't have a living category, traditionally.'

Bethany glanced at the foliage she was slowly being

pushed into. 'What about Mr Quinn? What sort of spirit is he?'

'What?' Sir Stoames asked, his head no longer visible through the branches. He sounded suddenly suspicious.

Bethany immediately regretted asking the question and realised how obvious it sounded. She didn't want to get Mr Quinn into trouble: he was the only one that had noticed the garden gnomes and he seemed to know something was wrong in Stagtree Knoll. 'I just meant, there were spirits in front of me when I came into the hotel. I was wondering what they were.'

'But why Quinn particularly?' Sir Stoames asked.

'Oh, no reason. I just heard you use his name. He was in front of me, that's all, and he looked odd,' she said innocently.

There was a brief pause as if Sir Stoames was contemplating something. 'If you must know, Quinn is a pooka. A spirit of mischief. A terrible order, related to leprechauns. Stay away from them is my advice.' He paused again. Bethany couldn't see his face but she was sure it would be frowning. 'He didn't have anything to do with you stepping out of your body, did he?'

She thought quickly. 'I just followed everyone else in. Maybe something's broken with the hotel.'

Stoames murmured doubtfully. 'Maybe,' he conceded. 'It should be easy enough to find out. Although this is exactly the sort of thing I would expect from Quinn. He's caused nothing but trouble since he arrived here.'

Bethany's attention shifted to her seat. She dodged out

of the way of a branch as she was pushed further up. She wondered how they were going to get down. 'We seem to be quite high up now,' she said a little nervously.

'What? Oh, that. Well, it really wouldn't take as long if you didn't keep interrupting. I'm the one supposed to be asking the questions.'

She clutched at the sides of her chair. Leaves stroked her face as she moved upwards. 'Okay.'

'So . . .' Sir Stoames consulted his sheet of paper. His voice sounded muffled. 'Do you have any phantom pets or guardian angels you might have brought in with you?'

She once had a pet gerbil that had escaped into the walls of her old house but she couldn't ever remember having a guardian angel. 'Not that I know of,' she said.

'Not known,' Stoames echoed. He sounded exactly like someone lost in a wood. 'And lastly, how did you find out about the hotel?' he bellowed across.

Bethany felt the darkness closing in. The legs of the chair had swollen into sturdy trunks and were pushing her up rapidly. It made her queasy just looking down at the office floor. 'When I saw you giving tours around the village.'

She was almost in complete darkness now. Her breathing came in quick bursts as she became panicky. She was ready to start shouting for help when rays of light cut through the darkness above her. Her chair thrust her up through one last layer of thick leaves and she found herself looking out across the treetops. She was relieved to see four walls enclosing the miniature wood and a ceiling above her painted a bright gold. It made the bushy trees look like an extremely lumpy green carpet.

Stoames emerged from a patch of leaves. He was covered in twigs and he brushed himself down and rearranged his tweed hat. Graceson clambered out of some nearby branches, panting with exhaustion, his glasses hanging off one ear. He was just in time to receive the sheet of paper handed to him.

'Well, that all seems to be in order,' Sir Stoames said as he got up from his chair. He began to casually walk over the green treetops and he motioned for Bethany to join him.

Tentatively, she stepped out of her chair. She didn't want to fall down and hurt herself, so she prodded what had now become the floor with her feet. It felt surprisingly firm and springy. Graceson held out a hand to steady her and she managed a few steps forward.

'So why are you giving tours round our village?' she asked.

Stoames shrugged. 'Spirits love being submerged completely in a body in the physical world. It's a novelty to them and is one of the unique experiences we can offer during their stay with us.'

Bethany tried to keep up with him, although it was difficult as she was having so much fun bouncing and swaying on the floor.

He clasped his hands behind his back and headed towards a green door on the far wall. 'Now, as I mentioned before, there are rules. It is important to remember and obey these rules at all times without question.

'Rule one: Always expect the unexpected and sometimes unexpect the expected.

'Rule two: There is no rule two.

'Rule three: If at any time you find yourself in difficulty, think of your favourite colour and sing your favourite song.

'Rule four, which used to be rule two: Do not, under any circumstances, attempt to discover his name, read or write his name, and especially speak his name aloud. All of which will be impossible as it is protected by dozens of forgetful spells. But don't bother trying even if you're extremely curious. It will end in your certain doom.

'Rule five: Rule four <u>underlined</u>.

'Rule six: Do not make duplicates of yourself.

'Rule seven: All bills must be paid promptly. Failure to do so will result in immediate loss of all privileges and status as a guest.' A nasty smile broke across Sir Stoames's face at this rule and he shot a menacing look at Graceson, who shivered and began nervously rearranging his glasses.

'These are the basic rules,' Sir Stoames added. 'There are an additional seven hundred and fifty-three rules covered in the rulebook of which you can obtain a copy by applying in writing to me. If you break any of these rules you become the sole property of the hotel. Is all that clear?'

'Wait, what do you mean sole property of the hotel?' Bethany said anxiously. She had a sudden vision of being forced to work in the hotel, picking up the luggage like one of the harassed ghosts. 'And how can I pay a bill? I don't have any money.'

Sir Stoames shrugged his shoulders. 'We accept all sorts of payment for our services, but in your case it will have to be a straightforward exchange of work. That is, of course, unless you can trade in magic?'

'What? But I can't do magic and I'm too young to work,' Bethany protested.

Graceson ruffled his papers. 'Is that an altogether good idea, Sir? I mean, where were you thinking of putting her?'

Sir Stoames stroked his moustache and gave a smug grin. 'Actually, I was thinking of the kitchens. The chef always needs help.'

'The kitchens?' Graceson trembled so much that his glasses slipped off his long nose and clattered to the floor.

'What's wrong with the kitchens?' Bethany asked quickly.

'Nothing. Nothing at all,' Sir Stoames said, shooting Graceson a look. He waved his cane in the air and opened the green door. 'We'll drop you off with the chef, come back for you when the portal is open, return you to your parents, along with a few forgetful spells, and no one will be the wiser. Marvellous!'

Bethany ran in front of him and blocked his path. 'What about my shadow and my body?'

He inspected her for a moment with a look of bemusement. 'I wouldn't worry about your shadow. The shadows are part of a very complex jinx that we use on all our guests. It's useful to keep an enchanted likeness of you in case you get . . . lost. As for your body, it is safe and will be returned when it is time for you to go back.'

'I want to go back *now*,' Bethany said forcefully.

Sir Stoames very deliberately tapped the golden plaque on the wall above her head. 'Do you see this?' he asked.

J's hotel for ghosts, spirits and non-material beings.

Bethany nodded her head slowly.

'This hotel caters for every sort of spirit there is: Undines, sylphs, salamanders, dryads, fauns and gnomes. We have city spirits, dream spirits, nymphs, sprites, pixies, nebbishes, pookas, shades, nightmares and daymares, demons, an angel or two, and on very special occasions, we have deities. But never living children. Ever. Do you understand?'

She nodded a second time.

'You've stepped over into the spirit world – something, incidentally, you shouldn't be able to do – and you can't just wander back whenever you feel like it. The portal to the human realm isn't open until tomorrow and that could be a long way off. So I suggest that you make the best of it.'

'What do you mean a long way off?' she asked.

He waved a dismissive hand in the air as if he were shooing away a fly. He stepped past her and walked back through into the original corridor they had entered the office from. 'Time is like everything else here. It doesn't obey the rules you are used to. You'll learn that. It stretches and shrinks and moves in all sorts of directions it doesn't in your world.'

Bethany followed sulkily as they began the long, tedious journey round the identical corridors. 'Is that why none of the clocks work properly here?'

'The clocks work perfectly well. They tell you what sort of time you're having, not what time it is.' He grinned and gave a flourishing tweak of his moustache. 'You'll find that's a lot more helpful.'

Bethany had a good idea what time one of those clocks

would be pointing to now.

As if sensing her frustration, Graceson piped up. 'It's sort of like . . .well, like dream-time, I suppose. You know how sometimes you have a dream where it feels like ages has passed but when you wake up hardly any time has passed at all? It's the same principle here.'

A slow, horrible realisation formed in her mind. 'So I could be stuck here for ages?'

'Just enjoy yourself and try not to think too much and everything should go fairly quickly. That's the trick,' Stoames said as way of reassurance. He strode round the next corner then stopped so abruptly that Graceson and Bethany both bumped into him. 'But if you begin to worry and make trouble and ask too many questions . . . well, then I'm afraid time will go by very, *very* slowly for you.'

Almost immediately Bethany started worrying about her parents and wondering whether they were still watching *What About Dave?* Had it finished by now? Would they be looking for her or would they even notice she was gone? She knew they were hypnotised, but she was sure it couldn't affect them so much that they would forget entirely about their daughter. Then again, who knew what powerful magic was at work?

She tried to push the thoughts away, but she could not have been doing a very good job as they all seemed to walk round the endless loop of corridors for an extremely long time. It was only when she was completely fed up that Stoames found the door he was looking for. They must have passed it a dozen times and Bethany couldn't help thinking he might have done it on purpose just to prove his point.

He began beating the door with his cane. His face screwed up with intense concentration as he pounded out a long and complicated rhythm. There was a pause, a discreet clicking noise and the door swung open. A wave of heat and noise blasted the three of them. There were screams and panic and a scene of complete pandemonium.

'Ah, yes,' Stoames said thoughtfully to himself. 'The kitchens.'

CHAPTER FIVE

THE HEAT OF THE KITCHEN

Bethany didn't want to enter the kitchens. They were so large and noisy and full of chaotic activity that it felt safer staying where she was. In front of her was a massive row of stoves that seemed to run in an endless line along one wall. Ghosts dressed in chef uniforms were running up and down it, checking the oversized pots and pans that filled every available space. To the left was a preparation area where teams of ghost chefs worked away at long, cluttered tabletops, running back and forth to fetch ingredients ready to be scrubbed, washed, chopped, mashed and peeled. Further along was a dishwashing area where ghosts were trying to clean the blackened pans piled up around them in tall, teetering towers.

The head chef stood on a raised platform in the centre of the kitchen, overseeing proceedings. He stuck out immediately from the rest of the staff as he was clearly some sort of fire spirit. His body was made up from lumps of black coal and he stood no taller than Bethany. His face and chef's uniform appeared in the flames dancing across the coal body, flickering and surging as he shouted out a continuous tirade of orders. The ghost chefs looked terrified of him and rushed from one task to another, spinning around, crashing into each other and occasionally falling to the floor. A clock on the wall wavered between *Hard* and *Very Hard* time.

'STIR THAT STEW! WASH THAT POT! FETCH THOSE FISH! STOKE THOSE FIRES! STRAIN THAT STOCK! FILL THAT PAN!'

A great deal of activity was focused around the gigantic pit that filled the centre of the kitchen. A group of chefs was heaving a pot as large as a bathtub off the end stove and carrying it towards the edge of the pit. They tipped the contents in. A thunderous rumble followed that shook the kitchen, sending equipment, food and ghosts flying into disarray. A fireball exploded from the hole and disappeared up an equally large funnel that hung above it like the roof of a marquee tent. It bathed everyone and everything in a wave of sizzling heat.

'Hmm. Seems quite organised here today,' remarked Stoames casually. He sounded vaguely disappointed. Graceson cowered behind the doorway, nervously glancing at the fire spirit.

'Maybe I could wait in your office until tomorrow,' suggested Bethany. 'I'll be very quiet.'

'Nonsense. You'll love it here. Kitchen work is character-building stuff.'

Bethany wasn't so sure. Looking around, the sort of characters it built were either exhausted or scared.

Stoames strode into the centre of the room and tapped the head chef on the shoulder with his cane. He turned and his body flared with flames as if he was about to burst into a nasty screaming fit. His red face cooled a bit at the sight of Stoames, taking on a more calm orange glow. He started shouting in a quieter, friendlier fashion.

'Ah, Jeremy. Goodtoseeyou. Goodtoseeyou! When are you going to get me some decent staff?! Look at them! Incompetent fools, the lot of them! YOU'RE ALL INCOMPETENT FOOLS!!!'

He waved a ladle at the ghost chefs who somehow managed to quicken their already frantic pace. Bethany was trying to block out the horrendous smell that had reached her nose from the unending row of simmering pans. Steam rattled the lids and gave off the stink of rotting, burning seafood. She felt her stomach flip and her body took on an unpleasant green hue. Graceson patted her on the shoulder whilst simultaneously ducking behind her back so that the head chef didn't catch sight of him.

'Actually, I'm glad you've brought up the subject of staff,' said Stoames. 'I've got a little helper for you here. Come over, Bethany. That's right. Don't be shy.'

As the head chef caught sight of Bethany the flames that made up his face fluttered as if a gust of wind was trying to blow them out. 'She . . . she's not a ghost,' he said, composing himself. 'What's the meaning of this? Bringing me one of the living? Have you lost your head, Jeremy? I mean . . .'

Stoames held up a hand. 'Just until the portal opens in tomorrow's real time. She slipped in. And if you help me out of this pickle then I might be able to put in a good word with *our generous host*. Maybe clear some of your bill, eh?'

This managed to silence the head chef as he considered. The flames danced less furiously. He smiled at Bethany. 'Why not? What harm can she do? I always need an extra pair of hands even if they are . . . *living* hands.'

'Marvellous. I'll pop by to pick her up when she's needed.' Sir Stoames turned on his heels.

'Good luck,' Graceson whispered in Bethany's ear. 'I'll make sure he doesn't forget. Don't worry.'

She wasn't sure what he meant by that but she didn't want Graceson to go – he seemed to be the only one that was nice to her. He gave her a reassuring smile before sprinting out of the kitchen after Sir Stoames. Bethany started to follow him and noticed the doorway was not leading back into the hallway that they had entered from. Instead, she could see them entering a room filled with banks of glowing machinery and dozens of screens. She stared at them intently. They showed different views of an unconvincing hospital ward and it took her a few moments to recognise the sets from *What About Dave?*

Stoames's voice trailed after him, low and conspiratorial. 'Graceson, I want you to try and isolate the broadcast and keep it transmitting into one house until tomorrow.'

'But isn't that dangerous? I mean, we don't know the

long-term effects of the device on —'

'Nonsense, nonsense. I'm sure it will be fine. The address is on the sheet I gave you, fifteen Stonebridge Road. Try and at least do this job properly.'

The door slammed shut behind them and Bethany felt a flood of panic. What were they planning to do to her parents? She instinctively went to open the door and follow them but stopped as soon as she noticed the head standing over her, glowering. His coal body glowed red and his flames became sharp and spiky as he resumed screaming.

'TOADEYE! LONGFOOT! GET . . . *LIVING-HANDS* HERE IN UNIFORM AND HAVE HER ON POT-CARRYING DUTY IN FIVE MINUTES! MOVE YOUR SORRY LITTLE LEGS! TURN THAT HEAT UP! MORE TRILOBITES! FASTER! QUICKER! MORE! MORE!'

Two ghost chefs stood to attention at the sound of their names. They rushed over and whisked her away to a supply cupboard before she could explain to the head chef that her name was Bethany, not Livinghands, and that she wasn't sure kitchen work was for her. A chef's jacket was swiftly thrown over her shoulders and she was helped into a pair of baggy trousers. The outfit started shifting and fluttering as if it was alive and adjusted itself to fit her body exactly, tightening and folding itself into neat creases.

'Hey! What's it doing?' she said in surprise. It was a ticklish sensation and she couldn't help giggling.

The taller ghost of the two with long, thin feet glanced at her unsurely. 'It'll help you find your way round the kitchen,' Longfoot said dolefully.

Bethany looked at the shorter, stout ghost who had unpleasantly wet, bulging eyes. He, too, seemed uncomfortable at her colourful appearance.

'Is the head chef always this mean?' she asked him.

Toadeye blinked several times and looked at the floor. 'Um, no. He hasn't been *this* mean for a long time.'

Longfoot nodded in agreement. 'Yeah, you're lucky you've caught him on a good day, Livinghands. Most of the time he's so mean he throws slow ghosts in the pit. Just for fun.'

'What?' said Bethany. She glanced over at the pit as it exploded with another ball of flames. 'Look, I need to get out of here and help my parents.'

The two ghosts looked back at her with complete incomprehension. 'Get out of here?' said Toadeye as if he'd never heard of the expression before.

Bethany thought of another way to explain it but her uniform began tugging at her as the head chef screeched for them to join the pot carriers. She followed Toadeye and Longfoot back into the kitchen and up the long line of stoves. The smell was unbelievably bad. Inside the cauldron-sized pans she could see all sorts of stews bubbling away, most of them containing either seafood or vegetables. The further along her uniform pulled her, the worse the smell got. The pans at the far end had black smoke pouring out and she got a peek at the dried, charred remains as one of the panicked chefs lifted the lid and stirred the contents. It made a noise like rattling bones.

Longfoot's feet slapped the floor behind Bethany's. Toadeye was running alongside her and whispered, 'Try and keep up. Don't make eye contact with the head chef. Or speak to him.'

They made it to the end of the stoves where the massive flaming pit sat. The heat was overwhelming at this end of the kitchen. There was a team of eight chefs, thin as rakes, all with disproportionately long arms. They had gathered around the last pot on the stove and were groaning as they lifted it up and moved it towards the pit. Toadeye and Longfoot joined them and Bethany felt her uniform guide her towards a place at one of the many padded handles. She struggled with the weight of the pan. Even with all the ghosts working together, it felt an incredibly difficult task keeping it upright. They could have easily been trying to lift an elephant for all the effort it took and she could see why the ghosts' arms were stretched out of shape. They grunted and shuffled forward.

Toadeye whipped the lid off the pan and a cloud of black, rank smoke smothered their faces. When it cleared, Bethany peered in to see it was full of an assortment of fossils, each hissing and popping with white-hot heat. She recognised the spiral shapes and cone shapes of small animals from biology books at school. There were chunks of dark stone with per-fectly preserved fish skeletons, and strange bobbled plants that might have been seaweed squashed flat like pressed flowers.

They reached the edge of the pit and with one final effort tipped the pan up. The fossils rumbled out and down and Bethany craned her neck to get a good view of their descent. Longfoot blocked her way, though, and she had to nudge past him to see what was going on down there, nearly tripping over his unnaturally long feet.

When she made it to the edge she almost fell over with shock.

The wide, gaping *O* of the pit went downwards like an enormous well. Filling this vast, dark space was a gigantic face. The sort of face that you might see carved into a mountain. It was covered in a thick layer of soot and its eyes shone out from the blackness, each one as big and bright as the moon. The nose alone was bigger than Bethany and the mouth looked like the opening of some deep, dank cave.

She felt dizzy just looking at it. She barely registered the mouth opening to receive the fossils that now seemed no bigger than a handful of crumbs. She was too transfixed by the giant's beard, which looked like weeds growing up a hill, to notice the deep rumbling. She had just realised how unhappy and angry he looked at being trapped in such a tight space when she was pulled backwards by the shoulders and a wall of flames rushed past her.

'Watch out!' cried Toadeye, as the giant's mouth exploded with fire. It singed them both as it surged upwards into the funnel. The force of the blast hurtled them thirty feet away on to the floor. They landed head over heels and both had to be helped up by the other ghosts. Toadeye's eyes were bulging so much that they looked ready to pop. He gave Bethany a look as if to say *that was close.*

'Well, I didn't know,' Bethany said defensively. 'I mean, why is there a giant in the pit in the first place? And why are we feeding him fossils?'

Some of the ghosts laughed nervously as if they weren't used to people asking questions.

Toadeye said, 'You have to feed a giant fossils. How else would we power the hotel?'

All the other ghosts nodded sagely as if this was the most obvious fact ever.

The head chef's screams rose in pitch. 'MOVE PANS SEVENTY-FOUR TO EIGHTY-SIX ONE SPACE ALONG! NO SHIRKING! TURN THAT HEAT UP!'

Everybody ran, rushing to the stoves to shift the pots along. Bethany followed Toadeye and stood in his way. It made her uniform bristle and tug at her forcefully but she wouldn't budge. 'But what's he doing in the pit?'

Toadeye glanced at the head chef. He was clearly unsure of how to react to this sort of behaviour. 'Well, um, he's trapped there. He has to be trapped to feed him the fossils.'

He tried to squeeze past Bethany to move a large brass pot shaped like an old-fashioned kettle. Bethany blocked him again.

'That's a horrible thing to do. Who put him there?'

He danced on the spot and his eyes were blinking rapidly. 'Um. *He* did. You know, *him. Our generous host.* Please, let me past. It's not like we want to do this, but we don't have a choice. We're only ghosts.'

He sounded so desperate that Bethany stood aside and let Toadeye rush to the kettle to lift it to the adjacent space. She helped shift more of the pots, feeling guilty for upsetting him. His arms were flapping about in a panic as the chefs struggled to move everything in time. No sooner had they shimmied all the pans along than they had to run to the end of the stoves and dump another load of fossils into the pit. Bethany was eager to get a better glimpse of the giant and positioned herself nearer to the edge.

This time, as the fossils tumbled down, she saw the giant's reaction. His eyebrows gathered into a scowl as the golden cords that held his head in place tightened, forcing him to open his mouth. It looked like he wanted to scream or bellow but instead he swallowed the fossils. His face grimaced as if he'd just been given unpleasant medicine. Then he began to shake violently against the sides of the pit, producing the dramatic rumbling that echoed throughout the kitchen. A deafening, flammable burp erupted from his throat and that was the point Bethany had to duck out the way.

The other ghosts turned back to the stove to continue their work but Bethany peeked over the edge to get another brief look at the giant. His face didn't show anger or hostility this time. His features had collapsed with exhaustion. The lids of his eyes fell and a single teardrop formed, as large as a crystal ball, and rolled off down his eyelash.

She felt bad for the giant. It didn't seem very fair. Bethany leaned as far over the edge of the pit as she dared to go. Her uniform pulled at her urgently to return to the other cooks but she ignored it. 'Hello?' she called. 'Hello,

Mr Giant. Can you hear me?'

It took a moment for the giant to realise he was being addressed. His eyes raised slowly before resting on the distant speck of light that was Bethany. Maybe it was because she was unlike the other ghosts with her colourful appearance that the giant's pained expression shifted for a moment. The constant scowl he wore changed to a look of curiosity.

'I don't know if you can understand me but I think it's wrong what they're doing to you,' Bethany called to him. She could hear her own voice getting louder as it echoed down the circular wall of the pit. 'Is there something I can get you?' She thought he might like something nice to eat after being forced to consume all the unpleasant fossils.

The giant's face grew more intense as it opened its mouth to answer. It tried to shape a word but something was stopping it from speaking and it became angry with the effort.

'Can't you speak?' she asked.

He tried to shake his immense head but even that was impossible as thick bands of gold were holding it in place.

Bethany had an idea. 'Blink once for yes, twice for no,' she shouted. 'Can you speak?'

Very slowly, the giant blinked twice.

Okay, she thought. It was a start, at least. 'Have you been trapped here a long time?'

He blinked his eyes once.

She couldn't understand why anyone would treat the giant this way to begin with but to do it for so long was horrible. *Why has no one helped him? What is wrong with them?* She felt upset and angry at the same time and it took her a moment to calm down before she could ask her next question. 'Can I help in some way?'

He blinked once.

'How?' Bethany shouted out before realising her mistake. She tried to think of a yes or no question but was distracted by the ghost chefs shuffling to the edge of the pit. 'No, wait,' she said, running towards them. 'Don't!'

They tipped another pan over the side and Bethany felt her heart sink as the fossils fell into the giant's open mouth. She turned angrily on the ghosts. 'Stop doing that! He doesn't like it!'

They were all taken aback at the force of her outburst. For a moment none of them dared move or say anything. Then the head chef started shouting, 'ALL CHANGE! ALL CHANGE!' Before Bethany could apologise to the giant she was being shoved away. Her group almost stampeded to the other end of the kitchen as they were relieved from pot-carrying duty. Toadeye and Longfoot each grabbed one of Bethany's arms and rushed her into the relative quiet of the preparation area. She scowled at them when they finally released her.

'It's for your own good, Livinghands,' Longfoot said.

'That's not my name!' Bethany replied furiously. 'It's Bethany. Anyway, I was trying to help the giant.'

Toadeye and Longfoot exchanged a nervous glance with each other and backed away out of hitting distance.

'But the head chef was looking at you. You really don't

want to get into trouble,' Longfoot explained.

'I don't care about that.' She growled with anger. She knew it wasn't their fault but she couldn't help feeling frustrated with them. 'I just don't want to be so scared that I let bad things happen! You could have stopped tipping the fossils in the pit!' she shouted at them.

As soon as the words were out of her mouth she realised how harsh she was being on them. Longfoot and Toadeye shuffled on the spot, clearly upset.

'No, wait. I just meant . . .' Bethany said, trying to think of some other way to explain her frustration.

'Just worry about yourself,' Toadeye muttered, hanging his head.

'Yeah,' Longfoot agreed. 'And for your information we're not —'

'YOU THREE, STOP SHIRKING!' the head chef screeched, his flames burning quick and bright with anger.

The two ghosts leaped up in fright and disappeared in different directions whilst Bethany's uniform tugged her towards one of the many worktops piled high with ingredients. She glared at the head chef, inwardly deciding that she was going to help the giant.

CHAPTER SIX

A DANGEROUS BUN

Bethany could see why the ghost chefs were so keen to work in the preparation area. It was cool and calm in comparison to the chaos of the pans and the pit. Tables groaned under the weight of strange ingredients – things that she had never seen before.

There were the trilobites that looked like freakishly shaped crabs, glistening mounds of them filling the vast sinks that lined one wall. Other shelled creatures were stacked beside them, ones with spiral shells, ones with long curled cones that she had heard a chef call nautiluses, ones with beautiful, colourful markings. Above the sinks were tanks filled with exotic shoals of fish that flashed silver as Bethany walked past them.

She decided to make her way to the piles of vegetables.

There were lumpy brown things caked with dirt and piles of broad fern-like leaves. There was a bundle of twigs and reeds that gave off pleasant aromas and a towering pile of a shaggy substance that oozed slime, none of which she recognised and she was fascinated by them.

Her uniform pulled and positioned her towards a long table. She resented being jerked about like a dog on a leash and deliberately pulled herself in the opposite direction so that she could help Toadeye peel a mound of carrots. She felt safer here, partially hidden from the head chef and near the one ingredient she was familiar with. She began to peel the vegetables, helped by the cuffs of the jacket that guided her hands to the pile.

'Where does all this stuff come from?' she wondered aloud. As she looked sideways she noticed Toadeye was deliberately ignoring her.

His eyelids fluttered nervously as he stared with unnatural interest at the carrots.

'I'm sorry,' Bethany said to him.

He glanced at her briefly.

'I didn't mean to shout at you. And you were trying to help me. I shouldn't have done that.'

Toadeye let his guard down. He smiled. 'You are quite feisty for a girl,' he said. 'I forgot the living are like that.'

They both giggled and Bethany thought she saw him surge momentarily with light.

'As for the ingredients,' he remarked with a knowing nod, lowering his voice, 'interesting thing that. We had an imp in here one time fixing the heating. He reckoned they can only come from one place and that's directly from the spirits. Vegetables from the vegetable spirits, fish from the sea spirits, animals from the animal spirits, and so forth. *Pure magical manifestations* which, if you ask me, is more than a little bit odd.'

'A little bit odd?' Bethany smiled. 'You're a ghost that feeds fossils to a giant in a pit wearing a uniform that drags you about. I don't think it could get more odd.'

'Point taken,' he said. 'It's just that a spirit giving away these things would be like you giving away your memories or your voice or your own happiness. It's what they are. It just doesn't make sense.'

They were both distracted as several chefs burst through the swing doors opposite them. They delivered fresh piles of vegetables to the tables and topped up the tanks with buckets of fish before disappearing back the way they came. Bethany caught a glimpse of another kitchen through the doors, as big as this one, only it appeared more organised and sedate. They didn't seem to be preparing fossils. In fact, it looked suspiciously like they were preparing sausages and almost all the ghost cooks in the preparation area were staring enviously into the other kitchen.

'That's the sausages!' Bethany said.

'Yeah,' Toadeye muttered longingly. A far away look entered his eyes. 'Sausage-maker. That's the job you want.'

'No,' she uttered, shaking him. 'That's what they're using to put my parents in a trance, that and the soap opera *What About Dave?*'

He looked completely blank and had clearly never heard of the TV programme. 'Right. But it's still okay to want to work there?' he asked.

'Not unless your plan is to sabotage all the sausages,' Bethany said threateningly.

'Um, right, yeah. It's just, well . . . It's always been a dream of mine,' he said sheepishly. 'They say if you work long enough and hard enough here then you can get a promotion to that kitchen.'

'Well, how long have you been here?' Bethany asked.

Toadeye's eyes rolled back and his lips twitched as if he was counting off numbers. 'I don't really know,' he finally admitted. 'I used to feel like I was here since forever but that seems so long ago now. It must be somewhere beyond forever.'

'Oh,' she said.

'I know.' He shrugged his shoulders. 'Time runs differently here.'

'Stoames told me that.' Bethany tutted. 'He also said I'll just make it worse by worrying or asking questions or anything like that.'

Toadeye nodded.

'But I think I should ask questions, like why have they trapped the giant in that pit? It doesn't seem right.'

Toadeye became embarrassed and unsure of himself at the mention of the giant. 'It's like I said before, you should just worry about yourself,' he muttered. 'You wouldn't be the first person Stoames brought here and forgot about, you know.'

'What?' The thought hadn't occurred to her that she

might not get out of the kitchen. 'What do you mean?'

'Originally, I was only supposed to be here to fill in for someone,' he explained in an offhand tone. 'Bert or Bernie he was called, or . . . no, wait a minute. That might have been my name.'

'But . . .' Bethany felt a creeping dread.

Longfoot, overhearing their conversation, smiled and sidled over. 'Yeah, Sir Stoames left me here to help out for a short while. Said he was going to come back for me and take me to a job in the hotel shop. That was a long, long time ago.'

She felt nervous and unwell.

Another ghost cook, called Floparm, joined in. 'I was supposed to be getting a job in the laundry. That was back when these were normal-sized,' he said, holding up his impossibly long, stretched arms.

More ghosts gathered around, eager to tell their own stories.

'What?' Bethany said in shock. 'You can't *all* have been left here? You can't *all* be waiting for Stoames to come back for you?'

Sadly, they all nodded.

Now she realised why Graceson had promised to make Sir Stoames return for her; it was because he never had returned for anyone else. *I'm going to end up just like them*, she thought. 'But . . . I need to get back to my parents! I need to get out of here and help them!'

Toadeye placed a calming hand on her shoulder. His bulging, sticky eyes took on a sympathetic expression.

'Come on, Livinghands. Don't you worry. You're one of us now. They might be able to crush our dreams and destroy our hope, but we're cooks and cooks stick together. They can't take that away from us.'

All the ghosts took it in turn to pat her on the back.

'NO STICKING TOGETHER!' the head chef screeched.

At once, the cooks scattered and left Bethany standing on her own, feeling worse than ever. She didn't want to be stuck in this kitchen. She didn't want to be like the ghosts. She wanted to be with her parents back home, laughing with them the way she had before they had fallen into a trance. She wanted things to be normal.

Bethany fell into a long, gloomy silence and time seemed to stretch out.

The cooks worked on and on, peeling, chopping and sorting. They all drifted into a bored routine and the silence was broken only when Longfoot began to whistle a tune to cheer them all up. One by one, the chefs joined in, each adding their own melody. Even Bethany whistled along with them and found it took her mind off things. The more they whistled, the faster the work seemed to go, until it felt like their bodies were doing the tasks automatically. Before long, Bethany and Toadeye had made their way through half of the mound of carrots.

Her hands became so accustomed to the task of picking and peeling carrots that she no longer had to concentrate on it. The whistling carried on indefinitely. She even started dozing at one point. Her eyes became heavy and her head lolled to one side. She let her thoughts drift away.

It wasn't like proper sleep, it was more like a trance where everything seemed to pass quickly and painlessly as she stopped thinking. When she concentrated once more on what she was doing her hands were still working away and she saw, with some surprise, that she had made it through the entire mound of carrots. Toadeye had moved away to help another cook catch some trilobites that were escaping across the floor. Bethany leaned down for the last carrot. Her hand stopped inches above it, though. The carrot was wriggling.

She rubbed her eyes and thought she must be day-dreaming.

The carrot wriggled again, jumped off the counter and rolled towards her foot. It stood up on its pointed end and bowed at her. She giggled and curtsied back. The carrot spun round and round in a blur, moving in such a whirr that little plumes of smoke drifted off it. When it stopped it had transformed into Mr Quinn.

'It's you!' Bethany exclaimed.

He put a finger to his lips.

'Sorry,' she whispered. She checked to see no one was watching them then leaned a little closer. 'You've got to help me.'

Mr Quinn grinned a grin that looked two sizes too big for his face.

'I need to get out of here,' she said. 'And I need to break the trance my parents are in.' She thought of the pit at the other end of the kitchen. 'And I want to help the giant,' she added.

Mr Quinn considered this with a quizzical frown. He lifted one hand into the air and clicked his fingers. A large cream bun appeared beside him. It had a round ring-pull in the top of it, like the pin in a grenade. He smiled proudly.

'A cream bun,' Bethany stated flatly. 'That's your answer?'

He nodded and, with a graceful bow, clicked his fingers again, twirled and disappeared.

'Great,' she sighed. She was disappointed that he had gone before she could ask him any questions, but she picked up the bun and placed it into the pocket of her jacket for later. It was a nice thought on his part, she supposed, although not exactly what she had in mind.

The head chef began shouting, 'ALL CHANGE! ALL CHANGE!' and everyone began rushing around in a panic. It was time to return to the stoves. Bethany followed Longfoot as he slapped his way up the line of cookers. Her uniform directed her to a pot that needed stirring, then along to another pot that needed topping up with spiral shells. Heat and noise blasted from the pit.

Through the babble of orders Bethany heard the head chef shout, 'NEXT PAN TO THE PIT, YOU USELESS FOOLS! THAT GIANT NEEDS FEEDING! THIS IS NOT A HOLIDAY CAMP!' An idea crept into her mind and she ran to join the team gathering around the end pot. They struggled to move it off the stove and they had to lower it to the ground and drag it along. Bethany clutched one of the handles and started pulling it with all her might in the opposite direction. The cooks looked at her with a mixture of confusion and anger. Grunting and groaning, they managed to get it to the edge of the pit despite her best efforts and, with a great heave, tipped it high enough for the fossils to fall out.

'You shouldn't do that,' warned Longfoot.

'Cooks stick together,' Toadeye reminded her.

The other cooks scowled at her and barged past her as they returned to the stove. Bethany didn't care. She wasn't going to help them make the giant suffer any more. Whilst the others moved the pans along she crouched down by the edge of the pit. Her uniform tugged at her urgently but she resisted. Something lumpy bounced around in her pocket as her chef's jacket pulled more insistently. *Of course, the bun!* It struck her why Quinn had given it to her now. It wasn't for her to eat, it was for her to give to the giant.

She waved both of her arms over the side of the pit to get the giant's attention. There was so much noise in the kitchen and so many orders being shouted out that no one heard her calling to him. 'Hello again, Mr Giant, Sir.'

His eyes shifted wearily and rested on the faint speck that was Bethany. A glimmer of hope lifted his features.

'Sorry about before,' she shouted.

His mouth opened and closed again as if he was trying to speak. The effort filled him with frustration and his eyes kept returning to Bethany as if there was something urgent he needed to share with her.

She removed the cream bun from her pocket and showed it to him. 'I thought you might like something nice to eat for a change.'

That cheered him up. His eyes glowed as he very slowly,

very deliberately blinked his eyelids once. Even his gigantic mouth quivered in anticipation.

Bethany examined the bun. She pulled the ring-pull sticking out of the top of it and immediately the bun began to inflate. Quickly, she aimed it at the giant's mouth, lobbed it down into the pit and watched as it fell down, growing in size. By the time it hit the giant's bottom lip it was as big as a beach ball and it rolled neatly into his open mouth.

The giant swallowed. His face strained with a powerful force. The expression of anger that he had worn for so long took a great effort to shift. His cheeks shook and stretched and finally broke into a wide, beaming grin that transformed his entire features, making him surge with light. A satisfying, non-flammable burp escaped from his mouth.

'Uuuurp!'

All at once, as if someone had given a signal, the entire kitchen went quiet. The head chef stopped screaming, the lids stopped rattling, the pots stopped bubbling, the chefs stopped running and whistling. Everyone and everything froze. A deep rumble, this one seeming to come from outside of the kitchen, rocked the entire building.

Bethany could sense the amount of trouble she was in by the number of shocked faces that turned to look at her. She tried to look innocent and casual but the faces focused on her were too stunned to react.

A siren suddenly sounded. The scene of complete silence turned just as abruptly into a scene of complete panic. The head chef's flaming face flared several feet into the air. 'FOSSILS INTO THE PIT NOW! ALL HANDS! ALL

HANDS! THIS IS NOT A DRILL!' Ghost chefs ran in every direction, tripping over one another, and those that weren't screaming were fainting in shock. Pans were being knocked off the stove. Someone spilled an entire tank of eels that wriggled across the floor, causing a pile up of chefs as they scrabbled towards the end of the cookers. The lights were blinking on and off, on and off, with the darkness getting longer with each flicker. The head chef flashed in red bursts like an emergency light.

Bethany thought she saw something very strange in that moment as the lights went off. It seemed as if the kitchen disappeared entirely and surrounding them all was an elaborate, swirling net of golden strands. It flashed for such a brief moment that she couldn't be certain of what she had just seen. Whatever it was slipped from her mind as a group of chefs managed to get a pot over to the pit and feed the giant his fossils. Finally, a mushroom cloud of orange flames burst upwards into the funnel and everything returned back to normal.

The lights came on and the panic was over. Chefs fell about like puppets with their strings cut. The head chef's face had disappeared in a blaze of white flames. His screaming had turned into an incoherent wail. Two ghosts were reviving him by taking it in turns to throw buckets of ice on him, which were immediately burning off into steam.

The door at the end of the kitchen opened and Sir Stoames came striding in. Graceson was flapping around behind him in a state of distress.

'What was *THAT*?' Sir Stoames screeched.

The ghosts had cooled the head chef's sufficiently for a hand to appear in the flames. It pointed to Bethany. Rather unfairly, she thought, as he didn't know all the facts. She smiled and shrugged her shoulders.

'Have you any idea what you've just done?' cried Stoames.

She tried to think of a way to explain how it had all come about but she found he wasn't too bothered with her explanation. He grabbed her by the collar of her uniform and marched her quickly towards the door.

Around the door golden thread was sprouting from the walls like strands of fine hair and Sir Stoames stared at them with mounting horror. They snaked across the floor to the pit, the ends of each strand peering like microscopes at the incriminating bun crumbs on the floor.

Graceson took Bethany by the hand as Sir Stoames hissed, '*Get rid of her!*'

She turned back just in time to see both Toadeye and Longfoot looking after her, their faces racked with worry. She waved at them and they raised their hands to wave back but a door slammed shut on the chaotic scene. The kitchen was replaced with the calm, quiet confines of a cleaning cupboard piled high with dirty mops, brushes and dusty shelves.

'How do you do that with the doors?' Bethany asked. She was busy removing the chef's uniform, which had finally stopped moving of its own accord, having given up trying to control her.

Graceson wasn't listening to her. He was concentrating

on the dingy room. Something was moving about in the murk, clearly disturbed at their intrusion. There was a scuttling sound and a blur of ghostly blue light as the thing ran up the wall and on to the ceiling.

Graceson's voice had risen so high it was breaking up. 'Muh-Ma . . . Maggie-Maggie?'

Bethany suddenly had a horrible lurching feeling as Stoames's last words rang in her ear. Get rid of her! She turned to Graceson. 'Look, I'm not sure what I just did but I'm sorry.'

He looked at her with a mixture of shock and complete incomprehension. 'What you just did? What you just did was manage to stop the power to the whole hotel. I've never seen anything like it . . . I mean, it's just . . . What were you thinking?' He shook his head. 'Anyway, it's a little late for apologies.'

Bethany's eyes darted about in a panic, trying to catch sight of the thing moving in the darkness. All she could make out was a multitude of arms and legs scuttling toward them. She clutched Graceson's arm and was about to plead with him to let her go when the thing dropped down from above them.

In the brief moment before the spider creature pounced at them, all Bethany could see was two heads, four arms and four legs . . .

CHAPTER SEVEN

MAGGIE-MAGGIE

. . . And two pairs of glasses.

The spider creature landed in front of Bethany and Graceson, except, as it straightened up, Bethany could see it wasn't a spider creature at all. It was the ghosts of Siamese twins joined at the hip. Two identical old ladies with long, thin faces and neat, bobbed haircuts shuffled forward. They were squinting through thick glasses that magnified their eyes.

'Ah, Maggie-Maggie,' Graceson sighed with relief.

'Oh, it's Graceson. Hello, luv,' said the twin on the right. Her wrinkles collected into a warm, friendly smile. 'How've you been? We haven't seen you for an age.'

The twins were clearly having difficulty in seeing properly as they strained to make out Graceson, even though he was standing directly in front of them. Their hands reached out to touch, pat and feel him, like a spider or crab examining an unusual object.

'We hope that Stoames isn't working you too hard,' said the Maggie on the left.

'Would you like a cup of tea, luv? Calm your nerves?' her sister asked. Her fingertips had detected the tremor in Graceson's shoulder.

He blushed a deeper blue and mumbled, 'Thank you. That would be nice.'

The twins moved to the far side of the cleaning cupboard. It was an impressive sight as they dropped down on their hands and feet and scuttled across, using each of their limbs to touch and move objects. They were surprisingly nimble for such old ghosts.

'We thought the power went out for a moment there,' one of them remarked. 'Gave us a funny turn, it did.'

They began to boil water on a little stove, set out some tin cups and measure out tea leaves into a pot, all in a sequence of fluid movements of arms.

'Oh, that. Yes. Well, funnily enough, that's sort of why I'm here,' Graceson said. 'You see, I have someone with me that —'

The twins' heads jerked up. 'A guest?' they cried together, and rushed back over. 'You should have said, dear. We thought we heard something. Who is it?'

Two sets of eyes struggled to see Bethany and it didn't help that they were facing the wrong direction.

'Hello,' said Bethany quietly.

The twins sidestepped over to her and began examining

her with their hands in very precise, gentle measurements. 'Why, it's a little nipper!' they declared. They sounded very pleased.

'Actually, I'm twelve,' corrected Bethany.

'Well, this is a surprise. This calls for biscuits. Tea and nice biscuits.' The twins scurried back to the stove, found another cup and removed an old tin box from the cupboard. They must have had extremely poor eyesight to have failed to notice Bethany wasn't a proper ghost, but she found it strangely reassuring.

Graceson's hands fidgeted, re-adjusting his glasses, fingers drumming his legs, scratching at his messy mop of hair. 'So, um, yes. I was just, um, wondering. Well, I was just wondering if you could take care of Bethany here for a little while? It's just that she's . . . well . . . not supposed to be here in the hotel. And we want to avoid *our generous host* from finding out about her.'

Maggie-Maggie handed out cups of tea and some stale, flaky biscuits. 'Oh, we'd love to take care of her, wouldn't we, dear?' said the right head to the left.

'We would, dear. It's been so long since we've had any company. Maybe she could help us on our rounds, eh?'

'Yes,' said Graceson cautiously. 'Maybe.'

Bethany sipped her tea and tried one of the biscuits. She was disappointed to find both had absolutely no taste whatsoever and she had to politely pretend she was enjoying them. Maybe ghosts just ate and drank out of habit, she thought, looking for a place to hide her cup.

'There's just one other thing,' Graceson said. 'Bethany

here is a . . . well . . . not a ghost. She's . . . um . . . sort of still alive.'

The sisters reeled back in shock and dropped their cups of tea. They gasped and tutted and shuffled forward to peer at her through their thick glasses.

'And she's not a spirit of any sort?'

'No,' Graceson replied.

'Or a demon playing a trick?'

'Unfortunately not. No.'

'Well, we've seen everything now,' one of them declared.

The other murmured in agreement and asked, 'How did she get in?'

'We're still not sure,' Graceson said, trying not to sound guilty. 'What is important is that we keep her out of the way until tomorrow when the portal opens again. I know I can trust the both of you.'

'Her parents must be worried sick,' said the right-headed Maggie.

Bethany felt glum at the reminder. She tried to block out the thoughts of her mum and dad trapped in front of their television. She felt confused and annoyed at what was happening. The twins patted her on the back and stroked her hair reassuringly.

'There, there,' said the left-headed Maggie. 'Mags will take care of you until it's time to go back.'

'Oh, thank you. Thank you!' Graceson said, clutching his hands to his chest. He edged towards the door. 'I'll be back tomorrow to pick her up. I really, really appreciate this.' Before he left, he glanced over nervously at Bethany.

'Please, try and not get in any trouble. It's for your own good. You'll just prolong things.'

Bethany felt her anger flare up. 'Wait! What about my parents? I heard what Stoames said to you, something about keeping the broadcast on them.'

He looked ashamed that she had overheard them and his hand reached for the door handle. 'They're fine,' he said unconvincingly.

'I thought you were being nice to me but you're not. You're just as bad as Stoames.'

Graceson winced at that. 'You don't understand. I'm just a g-ghost,' he stammered. He disappeared through the door before Bethany could say anything else.

She stamped her foot.

'I wouldn't blame Graceson, dearie,' left-headed Maggie said. Her sister nodded in agreement. 'That Stoames bullies him into doing all sorts. He's a sensitive soul, really.'

Bethany's anger deflated. Maybe she was being harsh on him, the way she had been on Toadeye and Longfoot. It wasn't their fault they were scared. They didn't know any better. Even so . . . she couldn't help feeling at least a little disappointed.

Maggie-Maggie started moving around in her spider fashion, moving up and down shelves and rearranging the stacks of boxes.

'Well, dear, I don't expect you'll want to stay in this boring cleaning cupboard for long and we've got work to do. Let's see. Let's see.' A foot tapped the ground as four arms rustled through a particularly dusty box. 'Ah, yes. Here we are.'

A smallish-sized cleaner's uniform was thrust at Bethany. She couldn't imagine a more boring job in such an exciting place and she began to wonder if it was possible to make it back to the kitchen and feed the giant again. Maybe if she could permanently stop the power in the hotel, she could escape. She reluctantly pulled on the outfit and felt it quiver and shift across her body. With a few quick tucks and folds, it fitted itself to her perfectly just like her previous uniform.

'Now, we just need to get a few things for the trolley,' right-headed Maggie said.

Bethany's uniform sprang into action. It gently guided her to the shelves and helped her pick out various cleaning supplies. She pulled down cloths, dusters, cleaning sprays and polish. She gathered fresh sheets and pillow cases that trembled at her touch just like her uniform. She took them to a square cleaning trolley and neatly sorted the items on to the racks. Maggie-Maggie was carefully placing silver canisters into a line on the top rack.

'Right we are,' left-headed Maggie said as she slotted the last canister into place.

Right-headed Maggie turned to Bethany. 'You push the trolley and follow us, dear. Try and stay near at all times. The hotel has a way about it sometimes. Doesn't like strangers.'

Maggie-Maggie went to the door and Bethany understood a little better how they worked. When they turned the doorknob, Maggie-Maggie did a combination of turns. Left, left, right, left, right, right, right, left. There was an upwards surge as if they were in an elevator and rising very quickly. It halted with a judder and Maggie-Maggie opened the door on to a luxurious, pink hallway. A plaque on the wall read: *Floor 303.*

'How big is this hotel?' Bethany asked in surprise. From the outside, it certainly didn't look like it had over three hundred floors.

'Hard to say for sure, dear. It's growing all the time. And, of course, bits get forgotten, too.'

'Forgotten?'

'Oh, yes,' the twins replied. 'Whole floors just get forgotten and disappear. Guests forget about certain rooms and it's not long before the rooms forget about themselves. They just sort of shrivel up and drop off. But there's always something there to take their place. Come along, dear. This whole floor was full last night. You can't imagine the mess some of the guests make. It's a miracle we can keep up with it.' They both tutted.

'Last night? But how can you even tell if it is night or day here?' Bethany asked. She still hadn't seen any windows anywhere since she'd arrived.

'Well, dear. It depends what it feels like. If it's night in one part of the hotel it's bound to be day in another part.'

'But that doesn't make . . .' She sighed with exasperation.

Right-headed Maggie smiled. 'Sense?' She patted Bethany's shoulder reassuringly. 'It's more like having the memory of days and nights here. We're not in the physical world where the sun rises and tells you it's daytime. We're in the spirit realm where time moves differently. Mostly it's

89

the ghosts that end up bringing a sense of time with them. Out of habit, I suppose.'

Maggie-Maggie hurried up the corridor. Bethany followed with the trolley, giving cautious sideways glances to the golden spirals of the wallpaper. The sisters seemed to know quite a lot and it made Bethany curious. She tapped Maggie-Maggie on the shoulder and whispered, 'Have you ever met . . . *him*?'

The twins considered. Two sets of eyes crinkled with concentration. 'Maybe. He probably made us forget about it, though.'

'He can't be very nice,' Bethany said.

'Why do you say that, dear?' asked the head on the left.

Bethany tried to keep her voice quiet even though she felt like shouting out. 'I was in the kitchen and there were all these terrified ghosts and a giant trapped in a pit and they were forcing it to eat fossils and one of the cooks told me that *he* put the giant there. And the giant couldn't even talk or anything. It was horrible.'

For a moment, there was a look of recognition in the twins' eyes. 'Oh, now. The giant. Yes. Very powerful spirit. One of the guests told me something very important about him . . . What was it?' They strained to remember something. 'No, no. It's gone.'

Before Bethany could explain that she wanted to go back to the kitchen and help the giant, the door beside them opened and made a loud, yawning noise. The doors on either side also stirred, opened and yawned.

'Ah. The rooms are waking up. We better get to work,'

right-headed Maggie said.

Bethany dutifully followed the sisters into the first room. She hated cleaning and tried to stall for time by pretending one of the wheels was stuck. Maggie-Maggie scuttled forward and began their chores, which involved a quick search of the interior.

The bedroom looked like a relatively normal hotel room with a wardrobe, bed, mirror, lamps and adjoining bathroom. The first thing that stuck out, though, was how miserable everything looked. The furniture sagged, the light fittings dropped their heads in despair. There were even decorative flowers interspersed with the golden spirals on the wallpaper that had wilted and were shedding petals.

'Oh, dear. There must have been a very sad spirit in here,' the twins muttered. Both heads turned to Bethany. '*Laugh*, please.'

Bethany looked around her as if there was someone else the twins might be addressing. She shifted uncomfortably and reluctantly stepped forward. She assumed the position of someone about to give a musical recital and realised, rather glumly, that she would never understand this place. *Think of something funny*, she thought. And, without thinking of a single funny thing, she started laughing. It sounded very fake and maybe that was why Maggie-Maggie was looking at her so strangely. 'Hahaha hahaha hahaha.'

The twins held up their hands to stop her. Right-headed Maggie said very calmly, 'No, dearie. *Laugh*. It's in the second canister to your left.'

Bethany looked down to the trolley. Sure enough, the

line of metal canisters were labelled: *Hide, Remember, Laugh, Calm, Dry* and *Extinguish*. Each had its own distinctively-shaped lid so that Maggie-Maggie could identify them by touch alone. 'Oh, right,' she said, blushing with embarrassment. She passed over the *Laugh* canister which had a lid formed into a wide grin.

Maggie-Maggie unscrewed the top and measured out a single drop of the liquid from the stopper in the cap. The sisters carefully tapped it on to the floor.

The room quivered as the liquid drained into the carpet. The light fittings were the first to giggle. They made a tittering noise that jiggled their lampshades. This set the wardrobe off and it banged from side to side as it guffawed. The curtains snickered like someone sneezing into a handkerchief. The bed thumped the floor. Everything convulsed with laughter until gradually the objects began to brighten up.

By the time the laughing fit finished, the room had transformed into a pleasant, welcoming interior. Now this was the sort of cleaning Bethany could enjoy. Her uniform tugged her towards the bed where she removed the old sheets and replaced them with clean ones, although the sheets did most of the work, tucking and folding themselves neatly around the mattress.

'Next!' cried Maggie-Maggie as they crawled away.

The next room looked as though it had flooded. Furniture floated in several feet of water and the walls and ceiling sagged with damp.

'Water nymph,' Maggie-Maggie decided.

Bethany immediately found the canister labelled *Dry* and handed it over to the twins. They shook out a small lump like a sugar cube and dropped it into the water. It immediately began to absorb the liquid and it started to swell and grow. After a few moments, with gallons and gallons of water having been soaked into it, the little white sponge was no bigger than a brick and the room was bone dry.

'Do all spirits leave a trace of themselves behind?' Bethany asked, intrigued.

'Of course, dear.' The sisters moved off. 'That's what makes a spirit a spirit.'

They quickly fell into a routine. Bethany would push the trolley up the corridor whilst the twins would inspect each room, scuttling about and prodding the furnishings to get an idea of what was wrong with the room. Then they would shout out for the supplies they needed and Bethany would leap into action. There were all sorts of strange scenes waiting for her when she entered a new doorway. At one point, she thought she heard Maggie-Maggie trip and fall. They screamed out, '*Remember* spray. Fetch the *Remember* spray – quickly!'

Bethany grabbed it and ran in after them and soon found herself falling down into blackness. The only light she could see was the square doorway getting smaller as she fell down and down. It seemed, after what felt like several minutes, that she would keep falling indefinitely. Maggie-Maggie appeared by her side, spread-eagled, like a bizarre, ghostly parachutist. A hand reached over for the *Remember* canister.

The sisters removed the cap and sprayed a generous mist all around them.

A faint outline of a room appeared. It gradually gained definition as a bed and wardrobe and curtains materialised. Before Bethany could figure out what was happening, she fell on to the springy mattress and bounced on to a solid floor.

'Weird,' she muttered. She went to help Maggie-Maggie up, since they had landed in a messy pile of limbs. The room was completely restored.

'Oooh,' said the sisters. Their faces had become animated and lively. 'That's right,' said the head on the left. 'You were asking about the giant. Yes, of course. It's amazing we forgot.'

The other head took over in an excited tone. 'Yes, yes. It was one of the older guests who told us. Apparently, Jickolass . . . Jaccobuss . . . Jocka . . . *he* trapped the giant in the pit and stole his tongue.'

Bethany was surprised at the sudden change in the sisters and realised that the spray must have affected them. They somehow seemed younger and more alert. 'Why would he do that?' she asked.

'Ah, well. Giants are very powerful spirits, you see. No one likes to get on the wrong side of them. And it must have known his name and been able to speak it. That's probably why *he* stole the giant's tongue, before it could name him.'

'What's so important about his name?'

The sisters tried not to laugh. 'A spirit without a name cannot be brought to answer. It cannot be confronted. It remains secret, unknowable, and ultimately, very powerful. All it would take is someone to say his name and . . .' The twins' attention shifted and a glazed look came over them as if they had lost the thread of their thought. Both Maggies began to chew on their lips and their eyes searched the air for clues as to what they were about to say next. 'Nope,' they said together. 'It's gone.'

'Try and remember. Please,' she urged them. The effect of the spray clearly wasn't as permanent on ghosts as it was on the room and Bethany could see it wearing off them. Their expressions clouded over and they scuttled off to their next chore. 'I need to know. What happened to the giant's tongue? It's important,' she shouted after them.

'Come on, dear. We've got a lot to get through,' Left-headed Maggie called back to her.

Her uniform hurried her back to the trolley where she put the canister back in its place. Bethany was thinking about what the sisters had said. It was like a light going on in her head. She now knew why the giant was so important and why she was right to want to help him. He was the key to everything.

Bethany idly tapped the *Remember* canister, wondering what else the sisters knew. It was important to get their help because she thought she had just come up with a plan to stop the hotel. And that, in all probability, was a bad idea.

CHAPTER EIGHT

THE TROUBLE WITH LAUGHTER

The next room shrieked and rocked with noise. Perforated lines of light glittered in the air. Strange, elaborate designs appeared briefly. The walls and ceiling were grimy with stains. What appeared to be piles of confetti gathered in small snowdrifts in the corners. Whatever had occupied the room had been large and complicated and very, very messy. Maggie-Maggie scuttled from one job to the next. Bethany brought in as many supplies as she could carry.

The twins sprayed and dusted, brushed and mopped. Bethany attacked a filthy part of the wall with some polish and a cloth. She scrubbed hard but, as soon as the stains seemed to have disappeared and she moved on to the next section, the grime would reappear, darkening the wall.

'You'll be there all day, luv,' right-headed Maggie said.

'Try the *Hide* canister,' suggested her sister.

Bethany retrieved it from the trolley. She sprayed some of it on to the wall and brushed the area with her cloth. The stains instantly vanished. Bethany found it very useful and started applying it generously across the walls. It was fine until she used some of the spray on a lampshade and half of it disappeared entirely. 'Oh,' she said.

Her uniform took her back to the trolley and guided her arm to the *Remember* spray. She used a tiny bit of it on the lampshade and, sure enough, it became whole again. She felt she was getting the hang of being a cleaner and much preferred it to kitchen work.

'Have you always been a cleaner here, Maggie-Maggie?' she asked.

The twins were busy using a vacuum cleaner that sucked up all the phantom noises. They shut it off. 'Not always, dear. When we first came here we were . . .' Both heads frowned again. Their legs tapped the floor as they tried to recollect.

Bethany gave a little squeeze on the *Remember* canister and a fine spray drifted over in the twins' direction. Their eyes lit up.

'That's right! We were acrobats! We used to do evening shows. Oh yes, very popular we were too. It was more a place for ghosts than spirits back then, you know, before all the ghosts ended up working here. We had a wonderful suite we stayed in. The Black Widow, they called us. It was all like a dream. Then, well . . .' The right-head turned to the left. 'I think we had problems with the bill, didn't we, dear?'

Her sister nodded. 'Yes, dear. Too many nights in the restaurant. Too many nights ordering from room service. I told you we needed to tighten our belts.'

'Yes, well. We've had to work it off. It must have been quite a large bill.'

'Well, it wasn't me, dear.'

'You were the one that wanted to stay in the deluxe suite, dear.'

The twins began squabbling, both speaking at the same time so that it was impossible to hear what either of them was saying. Their voices began to rise in anger and Bethany had to shout loudly to get their attention. 'What about the giant's tongue?'

They looked over to her, momentarily confused. 'What, dear?'

'You said before that he'd had his tongue stolen,' Bethany reminded them. 'Is there any way to get it back so that he could speak again?'

'Well, I suppose . . . It might be in the hotel somewhere,' Right-headed Maggie mused.

'Really?' Bethany asked.

'Oh, yes,' left-headed Maggie said. 'A symbolic object like that would be difficult to destroy. Better off to hide it somewhere in case you ever needed it. Most likely to be somewhere with an unusually high level of magical activity. Why do you ask?' But before Bethany had a chance to answer them, both sisters reached the same conclusion. Their eyes widened with shock. 'Oh, no, dear! You can't seriously be thinking about trying to find it? Far too dangerous.

Absolutely not! We forbid it in every way.'

'I just thought . . .' Bethany muttered, not sure how she could explain it to the sisters.

They looked horrified. 'No! We shouldn't have even mentioned it to you. What were we thinking?'

She didn't like seeing them so upset and decided it was best to let them calm down before she tried to ask any more questions. 'Maybe we should get on with the cleaning?' she suggested.

That seemed to satisfy them, and after a short while Bethany noticed the effects of the spray wearing off Maggie-Maggie as they returned to their vague, myopic state once again. Their worried expressions disappeared as they forgot exactly what it was they had been talking about. Dutifully, the sisters picked up the vacuum and resumed cleaning.

Bethany's thoughts raced. *What if she found the giant's tongue? What would happen if he could say that single name?* She had seen what devastation a cream bun had caused so could barely imagine what returning his voice to him would do. It was just a thought but a tantalising one all the same. Dangerous, she knew, from Maggie-Maggie's reaction, and foolish too, but still irresistible.

They continued cleaning the room. When the stains on the wall had been finished it was time to start on the piles of confetti. They resembled miniature heaps of rubbish and it took Bethany ages to brush it all up. 'What spirit caused all this?' she asked, noticing how exhausted it made her feel. They were spending far longer cleaning here than they had in any of the previous rooms.

'City spirit, dear,' said the twins.

'It's such a mess.'

'I know. And there are more of them every year. It wasn't like this in the old days.'

As Bethany swept away the rubbish, she slowly revealed a large mouse hole in the skirting board. Carefully, she cleared around it and found a message on the wall in tiny green writing. *You are all being tricked*, it read. It seemed a peculiar message and an even more peculiar place to write a message. 'Maggie-Maggie, I think I've found something. It looks like there've been mice in here.'

Maggie-Maggie scrambled over to the mouse hole. They didn't seem to notice the message written by it, or were purposefully ignoring it as their hands examined the edges of the hole.

'Leprechauns!' both sisters spat. 'We'll need the *Close* spray.'

Bethany paused before retrieving the can from the trolley. 'What about that message?' she asked. 'What do you think it means?'

The sisters both frowned and kneeled closer to the hole. 'What message?'

Bethany pointed directly at it. It was barely a few inches from their face. 'That message.'

'Hmmm. It looks like some sort of gibberish to me,' left-headed Maggie declared.

For the first time Bethany wondered about the sisters glasses. Why did they wear them when they seemed to have so little effect? 'Have you always worn those glasses?' she asked.

The twins looked bewildered, the sort of idiotic bemusement that was familiar from the village, as if they had never thought about their spectacles before. 'No,' one of the twins said eventually. 'I think we were given these when we started working here.'

'Really?' It didn't make sense to Bethany. Sir Stoames certainly didn't seem to care about his staff's well-being so why would he give Maggie-Maggie glasses? 'Can I have a look at them?' she asked.

Before Maggie-Maggie could protest Bethany was removing the glasses from left-headed Maggie's face. It wasn't easy. It felt like she was trying to remove a strong magnet. She had to grab hold with both hands and pull them with her whole weight just to lever them a few inches from her face.

Right-headed Maggie was saying, 'No, no, dear. I'm sure they're fine.' But left-headed Maggie let out a gasp.

'Well, how about that?' she exclaimed.

'What is it, dear?' her sister asked nervously.

Left-headed Maggie's eyes blinked in disbelief. She looked round the room, focusing on each and every object. 'Well, dear,' she said breathlessly. 'I can see perfectly clearly.'

'But that's impossible, dear,' replied her sister, in an equally shocked state.

Bethany tried to keep hold of the glasses but they were too strong and they sprang back on to Maggie's face. 'I think these glasses are cursed or something,' Bethany said. 'Maybe there are things the hotel doesn't want you to see when you're cleaning up.'

'I'm sure there's a reasonable explanation,' protested right-headed Maggie.

Bethany was about to try the same thing with right-headed Maggie to show her it was true, when she noticed the wallpaper coming alive with motion. The golden strands began to unspool from the surface. Had they sensed that she had interfered with Maggie-Maggie's glasses? She thought how terrified Sir Stoames and Graceson were of the moving threads and decided it was best to hide as quickly as possible. She wasn't sure what they would do to her for interfering with Maggie-Maggie's glasses but it couldn't be good, so Bethany jumped underneath the trolley and lay as still as possible.

The twins suddenly paled and pretended to be doing dusting. One head spoke to the other to give the impression that the sisters were talking to themselves. As Bethany held her breath, not daring to move even an eyelash, she wondered what sinister power the threads held. They were clearly in control of everything in the hotel and reacted when anything went amiss, but what were they were capable of that made everyone so scared of them? *Maybe now is not the time to find out*, she thought.

One thing she felt certain about: Maggie-Maggie's glasses must be cursed if it attracted the attention of the golden strands. It was becoming very clear that there was as much trickery and control of the ghosts and spirits inside the hotel as there was of the villagers on the outside.

Eventually, the threads settled back on to the walls and one of the sisters whispered, 'It's okay, dear. You can come out now.'

102

The twins looked a little different when Bethany emerged. The right-headed Maggie seemed cross, whilst her sister seemed more subdued. Bethany couldn't help noticing that they were a little clumsier as they moved furniture around the room. They were clearly shaken at the realisation that their glasses were hindering them rather than helping.

'You don't understand it here,' said the right-headed Maggie curtly. 'You shouldn't get involved in things that don't concern you.'

'But my parents —'

Right-headed Maggie held up the palms of her hands. 'Worry about yourself, dear. You're in a lot of danger. If he finds out you're here, he will keep you here. Had you thought about that?'

Bethany became very quiet. The sisters were right. That was the one thought at the back of her mind that she didn't want to consider seriously. It was stupid of her to risk being permanently separated from her parents.

Left-headed Maggie said, 'Don't worry about us, dear. We've grown rather fond of cleaning.'

'Now, let's finish off this room and we can all enjoy a nice cup of tea,' her sister added. 'I'll need that *Close* spray, please, dear.'

Bethany had a hollow, defeated feeling as she trudged to the cleaning trolley. She was miserable that there was nothing she could do. The sisters were being controlled by their glasses as much as the ghost chefs were being controlled by their uniforms. Much worse than this discovery, though, was their apparent lack of concern. They were just letting it happen.

Worse, now Bethany was letting it happen as well.

She felt angry with herself. She didn't want to be like the ghosts who were so scared that they didn't dare stand up to the unnameable *J*. What if she did do nothing like Maggie-Maggie said? What if she forgot all about her plan to find the giant's tongue? She might make it back to her parents and the village but the broadcasts wouldn't stop. And what sort of magic would be used on her to make sure she didn't tell anyone anything? The more she thought about it the more she felt strong and defiant.

As she looked through the trolley for the *Close* spray she noticed a canister that had not been there before. She frowned at the label. *Trouble*. Her hand reached for it and the solid canister dispersed in a cloud of smoke. Mr Quinn appeared, grinning.

'You!' huffed Bethany. 'Well, you've got one thing right. I get in more trouble every time I see you.'

The miniature Mr Quinn blinked and let out a gurgle of laughter.

'It's not funny. Stoames guessed it was you that let me into the hotel. *You* could be in a lot of trouble too.'

Mr Quinn seemed to consider this seriously. He leaned forward as if he was about to whisper something to Bethany. Unfortunately, he was standing on top of a canister and his movement made him lose his footing and caused the cylinder to turn. He tried to regain his balance but it just made matters worse. The canister spun round and round, gaining speed as his tiny legs ran on the spot. It rolled off the trolley, bounced on the floor and began to roll down the corridor, with Quinn's arms and legs wheeling as if he was about to go flying at any moment.

'Come back here!' Bethany hissed. She chased after him. 'I need your help and I don't want you disappearing on me like you did last time! I mean it!'

But Mr Quinn was out of control and the rolling canister built up speed, swerved into the wall and sent him hurtling up into the air. He came tumbling down and landed on the cap, which came free with a loud popping noise. A pink liquid glugged out of the opening and spread in a wide pool over the carpet. Mr Quinn surveyed the mess and looked up guiltily at Bethany. He smiled apologetically, clicked his fingers and disappeared.

The entire contents of the canister had drained into the carpet and Bethany now saw the label clearly. *Laugh.*

She felt a dreadful sinking feeling. Maggie-Maggie had only used a single drop in each room . . .

'Is everything all right out there, dear?' the sisters called.

'Um . . . fine,' replied Bethany, bracing herself. A sickening lurch ran down the length of the hallway. There was a deep tremor that seemed to shake the entire floor. Bethany tried to run towards Maggie-Maggie but the carpet and walls pulled backwards like stretched elastic. There was a *BOOM* and she was suddenly catapulted forwards on to the flexing carpet. The floor began to wobble underneath her and the walls shook, as if she was at the centre of an earthquake. A deafening banging sound accompanied each shudder. Furniture rattled in rooms and a deafening banging sound accompanied each shudder.

Bethany couldn't help screaming. She covered her ears and curled up into a ball as the contents of the cleaning trolley were scattered about her. When she dared to peek up at the corridor it was stretching and contracting in jerky spasms of motion, and she thought it was what the giant's throat might look like if he had a laughing fit. The golden strands squirmed at each thunderous blast and shrivelled as if stung. Lights shattered. Doors ripped off their hinges. The twins screeched.

As the tremors became quicker and more ferocious, Bethany was bounced up and down on the floor. Objects crashed by her side and she tried to grab a canister in the hope that she could undo the laughing fit. She looked around her and that was when she noticed the walls flickering like faulty lights. Except it wasn't just the walls. It was the whole corridor. Everything faded and became transparent, showing rows of rooms, which in turn flickered and became transparent, revealing more corridors and rooms beyond.

For a brief moment all she could see were the golden strands that permeated everything. They spread in splitting branches, making up the honeycomb structures of the rooms. They surrounded Bethany like a huge, elaborate golden cage. Deep inside it were glowing points of light, trapped, shimmering. Then the whole thing flickered again. Walls and ceilings returned. The corridor reappeared. The quaking slowed and faltered. Gradually, everything settled back into place as the liquid laughter wore off.

When it was safe to move, she pulled herself up from the ground. The contents of the trolley were strewn about her and one canister in particular had rolled towards her hand. She noticed the *Hide* spray.

Perfect, thought Bethany. She pulled off her uniform, picked up the can and started spraying herself. It was time to put her plan into action and make her own way through the hotel.

The threads were already returning to life and she heard a door slam at the end of the corridor and Sir Stoames shouting, 'WHAT NOW?!'

The stream of mist made her legs disappear, then her torso, her arms, her shoulders, until her whole body had vanished. She had no idea how long its effects would last but going by the *Remember* spray she thought it was best to saturate herself in it. She was just in time. Sir Stoames walked right past her, tapping his cane and muttering. 'What has she done this time? I knew keeping her was a mistake.'

His irritation disappeared as the golden filaments grew out of the wall. Their tips began to examine the empty laughter canister. Hundreds of them gathered around Sir Stoames, swaying and undulating like the tentacles of a sea anemone. He became nervous as they suddenly vibrated, moving in jagged shapes as if they were conducting an electrical charge.

'Yes, Sir,' Sir Stoames said.

The threads quivered again as if they were speaking. If they were, only Stoames could hear them and he looked very afraid of what they were saying to him.

'No, no. I don't understand it either. It seems like an accident but maybe it is a bit of a coincidence, as you say,

Sir. I'll speak to the cleaning ladies.'

The threads thrashed violently.

'Yes. I'm sorry to have disturbed you, Sir. I'll make sure it won't happen again.'

The gold retracted back into the walls and Stoames took out a handkerchief and mopped his sweating brow. Bethany quietly followed as he found Maggie-Maggie sprawled in the end room. 'Where is she?' he whispered as he helped the twins up.

Both sisters looked dazed. 'I don't know, dear. Isn't she with you?'

'She certainly is not. This is rapidly turning into a disaster.' Stoames tapped his cane impatiently. He briefly glimpsed the mouse hole and the tiny graffiti above it. His lip curled in disgust. 'Well, she can't have gone far.'

As he made his way back out into the corridor he nearly tripped over the *Hide* canister. He picked it up, read the label, then noticed the discarded cleaner's uniform at his feet. His head jerked up as the green door at the end of the hallway opened and shut by itself. He hurried to follow Bethany.

CHAPTER NINE

CONNECTIONS

Sir Stoames pursued Bethany through the door just as she thought he would. Except she hadn't gone through the door. She was still standing in the hallway, waiting for Stoames to lead the way.

She moved very quietly behind him as he entered a new corridor. This one was dingier, looking like a sort of maintenance area not meant for guests. It stretched a long way and was lined with different-sized doors, some as big as barn doors, some smaller than cat flaps.

He opened each in turn and looked inside, muttering under his breath. Bethany stayed close behind him, peeking through the entrances whenever she could. There were all sorts of strange places revealed. One door led to a restaurant where spirits were gathered around tables, their heads stuck in menus, although there was no sign of food anywhere.

Another opened into a tunnel that smelled of sewage. Several translucent slug-like creatures were digesting piles of waste. Yet another door opened to show a spacious swimming pool, but instead of water it appeared to contain a section of night sky, twinkling with stars, which spirits were gently gliding through.

The most interesting place was the last door that he opened, though. It led to a vast hall that billowed with steam. Various spirits were slumped in the long lines of bathtubs, wilting in the tremendous damp heat. Ghost staff patrolled the aisles, carrying long poles with nets attached to the end. From a distance they appeared to be using the nets to sift out objects from the bathtubs, which they were emptying out into large piles at the far end of the hall. What was peculiar about this was that the objects looked like all the ingredients used in the kitchen: lumpy vegetables, silvery fish, colourful shells.

It was an important enough place for Stoames to wander into. The ghost staff worked quicker in response to his presence, hurrying up and down the rows of bathtubs as he cast his critical eye over them. Bethany hovered at the open door then followed him in, making sure to stay several paces behind him.

Up close, she watched the spectacle of the bathing spirits with fascination, noticing that they looked as if they were asleep or in some sort of trance. The liquid they were submerged in did not resemble ordinary water but swirled and bubbled around them purposefully, pulsating with a luminous blue glow. The fluid seemed to draw out the light from the sleeping spirits, flashing brightly as it produced the objects that were being efficiently collected by the ghosts, a process that was causing the spirits to dim and flicker like faulty light bulbs. She remembered Toadeye saying they were giving up part of themselves and felt sick and horrified at what she was witnessing

In contrast, Sir Stoames murmured appreciatively at the scene. He stopped at a bathtub where a large sea spirit was shimmering. Several ghosts were gathered round the tub, removing the piles of trilobites and nautiluses emerging from the luminous liquid.

A snake spirit made its way towards him, slinking between bathtubs and stopping to instruct the ghosts where to go and what to do. It curled its long body up in front of him, its tongue flicking the air. 'Sssir Sstoames,' it said in a lisping voice. 'And to what do we owe the pleasssure of your company?'

He grinned insincerely at the snake spirit. 'I was in the area. Thought I'd pop in and check how you were doing. Everything fine, is it? No unusual . . . *interruptions* of any sort?'

'Interruptionsss?' the snake hissed.

'Yes. Any unwanted visitors?'

'Let's sssee,' the snake said, turning its head on its side as if in deep thought. It seemed to smile, revealing a venomous fang. 'There's only been you.'

Stoames grumbled. 'Never mind, never mind. How is the extraction coming along?'

'Most sssatisfactory.' It motioned with the tip of its tail at the busy hall. 'The sssea sssspirits and vegetable ssspirits are proving to be *most* productive, although we've not had so much luck with a couple of naiads.'

Sir Stoames surveyed the bathtubs and nodded. 'Well, just make sure to return some spirits to their rooms. We don't want to arouse too many suspicions. Keep the ones that are producing the most and . . . well, you know what to do. Extract everything you can.'

'Of course.'

Everywhere Bethany looked she saw the ingredients she had been using in the kitchen fished out from the sinister glowing liquid. One particular spirit, several rows across from where she stood, appeared to have had so much of its energy sapped in this way that there was barely anything left of it. A vague patch of light was all that remained. *It isn't just the giant that is being used to power the hotel*, Bethany realised. *The spirits are being drained of their magical essence without them even knowing.*

Her attention was drawn to a set of swing doors as two ghosts dressed in waiters' uniforms carried in a sleeping form that appeared to be a pixie of some sort. They lifted the spirit towards an empty bathtub and the snake hissed with satisfaction, uncoiling and moving off to instruct the ghosts. 'Do excuse me. I have fresssh deliveriesss.'

'By all means,' Sir Stoames said. He turned on his heels. 'It was just a flying visit.'

Bethany hurried back to the door as Sir Stoames returned to the corridor. She carefully positioned herself so that she was standing behind him as he closed the door on the hall and went to the door at the end of corridor. He whistled his short, three-note tune and turned the handle right three times, then left once. She memorised the combination and followed him as he stepped through into his office.

Graceson was running about under the trees, picking up paperwork that was scattered about the floor. The trees were shedding the sheets as if they were leaves in autumn.

'Well, this situation is just getting worse and worse,' fumed Sir Stoames. His nostril hairs quivered with indignation. 'She brought a fit of hysterics to the top floors and now she's completely disappeared.'

Graceson wrung his hands. 'I'm sure it won't be long before she's spotted. She is rather . . . conspicuous.'

'No. She's disappeared, Graceson. She used some *Hide* spray on herself and she went running into one of the connection corridors. I couldn't find a trace of her. She could be anywhere by now.'

Bethany had to hold back a giggle, then quickly checked herself to see if any part of her had become visible yet. She had to be careful. She had no idea how long the effects of the spray would last and being caught now before she had even explored the hotel would be disastrous, but she knew Stoames was the key to finding out more about this place. After all, he knew how it all worked.

Stoames threw himself into his chair with a weary sigh. The nearby clock was pointing to *Revealing* time. 'We could be in trouble if we don't find her. He already suspects something is going on.'

Graceson looked downcast.

Stoames scowled. 'I just don't understand it. I mean, she

must have been wandering about the village. That means she wasn't hypnotised by the broadcast. How is that possible, Graceson?' he demanded.

The ghost assistant flinched and shrugged his shoulders. 'Maybe she chose not to watch it?' he suggested.

'No. The sausages should have prevented any resistance. The chances that she managed to avoid the sausages *and* the broadcast are extremely remote. It's all very odd. Talking of which, how are the parents reacting to the broadcast?'

Bethany tensed up at the mention of her parents and had to fight the instinct to move closer or shout out.

Graceson rearranged his glasses. 'Um, yes, well . . . We've isolated it to the house and managed to keep them hypnotised. There have been a couple of unusual *fluctuations* that we can't quite explain. Maybe something to do with the temporal dissonance or the primer spell having weakened.'

'None of your gobbledegook, Graceson. Just make sure it runs smoothly,' Stoames said irritably. 'I want results, not excuses.'

The ghost assistant nodded meekly.

Bethany wondered what the fluctuations might mean. Was that good or bad for her parents? Maybe she should try and find the source of the broadcast and stop it. Or try and make it to the cloakroom and get her body back. Her thoughts raced. She knew that helping the giant should be her priority because that would mean stopping the magic responsible for all of her problems.

'Any sign of Quinn?' Stoames asked.

'Not yet. I sent his shadow after him but he's nowhere to

be seen.' Graceson returned to his task of picking up and sorting papers.

'It's all highly unusual,' said Sir Stoames. 'Suspicious, even. Yes. That's what it is. Suspicious. I'm almost inclined to believe it's an act of sabotage, that it's no accident she is here.'

'She is only a girl.'

'A girl, yes. But trouble nonetheless. Can you imagine what might happen if this keeps up? It's almost as if someone is purposefully trying to wake up . . . *him*. Well, whatever the reasons we need to find that girl and stop her. Even if it means . . .' Stoames let the threat hang in the air.

Graceson gulped and his ghost body dimmed a little. 'S-Sir?'

Sir Stoames fixed his assistant with a grave expression. 'I'm sure I don't have to spell it out, Graceson.'

Bethany felt herself go cold. *What was he suggesting? Would they keep her trapped here?* Or something worse? She knew it had to be bad if neither of them could talk about it and it was becoming clear how ruthless Sir Stoames could be. She eyed the door anxiously. *Maybe now was a good time to go.*

'I think this paperwork needs looking at,' Graceson said. He shoved a bundle of pages on to the desk and it managed to distract Stoames from his line of thought. His eyes lit up with greedy delight.

'More bills, eh?' He flicked through each sheet eagerly. 'Well, well, well. Looks like we might have a few additions to our happy team.'

Bethany had to fight the urge to suddenly run from the room. She wanted to be as far from there as possible but she had to be careful. Moving her legs incredibly slowly, she began creeping towards the door. She dared not make a noise, even if it did mean she had to move at an infuriatingly slow pace.

Graceson hovered over Sir Stoames's shoulder, nodding enthusiastically at each cheerful murmur. He looked a little more uncomfortable than usual.

'Actually, I was . . . um . . . just curious, Sir Stoames, Sir. I mean, well . . . how is *my* bill doing? You know, just off the top of your head. If it's no bother. I was wondering if I had worked it off yet?'

Stoames waved him away without looking up. 'I thought you told me you had sorted out the leprechaun problem. I found another hole up on floor 303. And some more were spotted in the restaurant. We're infested with them, I tell you.'

'Really?' gulped Graceson. 'Well, I sent out some ferrets but —'

'I tell you what, get me the girl and Quinn and I'll see about getting you some time off,' Stoames said, stretching back in his chair.

The ghost attendant visibly shrank. 'Oh, yes. Certainly. That would be, um, very generous.'

He walked towards Bethany and she froze, thinking that he had somehow noticed she was there. At the last moment she remembered to step out of the way as Graceson went to the door she had been moving towards. He opened and closed it after him before she had a chance to follow and she cursed herself for not being quick enough.

Sir Stoames shifted from his seat and looked over at the door. His mood changed instantly with Graceson out of the room. He became furtive and stealthy as he got up from his desk and sneaked towards the wall where the hotel sign glowed. Thinking he was all alone, he swiftly jumped up on a tree stump to reach it. This was clearly something only he knew about and that made Bethany curious. She edged closer.

He hummed a tune at the metal plaque. *Dum dum dee dum.* She recognised it as some classical music. Unseen mechanical workings clicked and whirred and the metal plaque opened outwards like the door of a vault. Bright golden light shone out from the secret compartment and Stoames gave a gleeful chuckle. He reached inside and pulled out a handful of bills and began to play with them as if they were huge sums of money. 'Ah, yes. There you are,' he muttered to himself. 'All my lovely little servants. Not so full of yourselves now you've got to answer to me, are you?'

He sounded slightly demented as he laughed to himself but Bethany wanted to see what else was in there and she eagerly walked forwards. She glimpsed piles of objects stacked up in the vault. There were bottles of potions that glowed mysteriously and sealed boxes with inscriptions on them like the canisters Maggie-Maggie used: *Charm, Control, Intimidate.* One of the bottles, she noticed, simply had the word *Tanglefinger* written on it.

So that's where he got his magic from, she thought. She

craned her neck to get a better look. There was a magnificent golden light being cast from several tiny pots at the centre of the vault and she had just noticed that the air above them was fizzing and sparkling in an unusual way. *Maybe this was the sort of place where you could safely hide an enchanted giant's tongue.*

She was so overcome by the urge to get closer that she barely noticed the twig snapping under her foot. Sir Stoames's head jerked upwards and Bethany took several very quick, very careful steps away from the broken twig.

He stealthily placed the bills back into the vault and slammed the door shut, then jumped down from the tree stump, nearly landing on her foot. His eyes scanned the room. She tried not to move a single hair or make the slightest noise, holding her breath. He was dangerously close to her, his head only a short distance from her own, and she was caught in an awkward position. He stayed very still and waited.

'If you're here, let me know,' he said in an unsure tone. 'You really don't want to make things any worse for yourself.'

Does he know I'm here or is he bluffing? she wondered. She turned ever so slightly to judge how far it was to the door when his gaze fell directly on her. He squinted at the air as if he could detect her faint outline and Bethany froze in fear. His hand reached out to her head and she realised with horror there was no way out, that she was about to be caught . . .

At that moment, mercifully, one of the trees shed a piece of paper and it made a rustling sound at the other end of the room as it landed. Stoames hesitated and Bethany crouched down as he looked the other way. He turned back and swiped the space where she had been. He sighed, disappointed, and his air of suspicion dropped. He walked over in the direction of the fallen paper, mumbling to himself.

Graceson returned moments later, standing at the open door. 'I've sent the girl's shadow out to look for her. It shouldn't be long before we find her again. Is . . . is everything okay?'

'Fine,' Stoames muttered irritably. 'Although it should be me that gets time off, I'm starting to imagine things.'

Bethany saw her opportunity, escaping past Graceson and out of the door just in time. He slammed it shut and Bethany collapsed against the wall of the corridor. *That was too close!*

CHAPTER TEN

LITTLE
PROBLEMS

She walked to the far end of the connection corridor before she dared to sit down and let out an almighty sigh. She tried to gather her thoughts. She just wanted to run as fast as she could but she had no idea where to run to. Maybe she could make it back to Maggie-Maggie and ask for help. The sisters might have a more specific idea of where to look for the giant's tongue if she sprayed them with more of the *Remember* spray. Or maybe she could go in search of Mr Quinn who did at least seem to have power against the hotel, even if it was unpredictable.

As she tried to decide what to do next she felt something scurry across her foot. It felt suspiciously like a rat. She squealed and shook her leg. The rat went flying, although as soon as she looked down to the ground there was nothing to be seen. She was just about to breathe a sigh of relief when she heard dozens of tiny feet scurry across the floor. Again she looked down and again could see nothing.

'What was that, Seamus?' said a high-pitched voice. It had a distinctly Irish accent.

Another voice to the right of her foot groaned and said, 'Not sure, but it hurt my head, so it did.'

Invisible Irish rats, thought Bethany. Why couldn't anything in this hotel be normal? She decided it was best just to get out of the connection corridor and find somewhere safe. As she edged herself along towards the far door her foot knocked another invisible body.

'Ow!' cried a third voice. 'Flannigan, it just got me too. Seamus is not wrong. It certainly likes to hurt heads.'

'Where's Donovan?'

'It wasn't me,' replied the fourth voice. 'I'm over here. Or at least I think I'm over here. Where are you?'

'Right,' sighed the first voice.

Bethany heard some more scurrying, then felt something bumping into her foot. It was followed by a sudden, sharp pain in her ankle as if she'd been stabbed with a pin. 'Ow!' she cried.

'Did you get it, Flannigan?'

'To be sure. It made a noise.'

'Well, get it again before it gets you.'

Bethany stamped her foot. 'Don't you dare get me again,' she said. 'I didn't mean to hurt you. It was an accident.'

The rats stopped moving.

'Show yourself!' shouted the first rat.

'Show me too,' added another.

'Shut up, Donovan.'

She peered harder at the ground but could still see nothing, even though she could sense tiny bodies surrounding her feet. She leaned down. 'I'm hidden. Why don't you show yourselves, that way I won't stand on you. I promise.'

There was a low murmuring and muttering as though the rats were involved in a heated discussion. After a moment, one of them announced, 'We'll show a little bit of ourselves and see how we feel about that.'

'Okay,' said Bethany.

Several small forms materialised on the floor. An eerie green glow began to form into the shapes of four tiny men, no bigger than Bethany's hand. Their faces were stretched into wide, rubbery grins, with large eyes that glinted with mischief, and low brows topped in mops of red hair. They appeared in patches so that only about half of each of them was visible. It was enough.

'You're not rats!' cried Bethany.

The bravest one stepped forward. This was probably the one that had stabbed her in the ankle, Bethany guessed. 'Why would you think we were rats? Can you not see with your own eyes that we're pure blood leprechauns?'

'You've only just become visible,' she said, defensively. Their tiny bodies made her think of one person. 'You're not friends with Mr Quinn, are you?'

A shock of recognition passed through the group and they vanished as quickly as if she'd blown out candles on a cake.

'She knows about Quinn!' whispered one of them nervously.

'Quiet now! She doesn't know anything.'

'But if she's seen him she'll know —'

'Shshshsh!'

'I'm sorry,' said Bethany. 'It's just you look a bit like him. I didn't mean to upset you.'

Cautiously, the leprechauns re-materialised – completely this time. The leader folded his arms. 'We've shown ourselves, now it's your turn.'

'I don't know how. I covered myself in *Hide* spray. I thought it would have worn off by now. Look, here's my hand.' Bethany reached out her hand to the leprechaun so that he could touch it. Each of the little men moved forward to examine it, making her giggle as their prodding tickled her palm.

'A spray, you say?' the leader said. 'You're not the brightest of things, are you? The magic they use in those sprays is meant for rooms, not for ghosts or spirits. The effects are completely unpredictable. Even Donovan knows that.'

'What's that now?'

'Shut up, Donovan.' The leader stroked his long chin. 'Seamus,' he called. 'Use some of your dust on her. Unhide her.'

A little bearded man removed a pouch from his belt. He stepped forward, pulled a handful of powder from his sack and blew it on to Bethany's hand. 'Bong-hige do-raity ahern.'

Bethany's arm began to glitter in patches and appear. Colour ran up from her hand to her shoulder, then to her head, and down towards her feet.

Four sets of eyes widened. The leprechauns 'oohed' and 'ahhhed' as she became visible.

'What is it?' asked one.

The leader said, 'I think it's a living ghost. Very rare. I've never seen one before.'

'My name's Bethany,' she said, leaning down to introduce herself properly. The leader shook her index finger.

'I'm Flannigan,' he said. 'That's Donovan, Seamus and Pat.'

Each of the leprechauns took it in turn to bow.

Flannigan folded his arms again once the pleasantries were over with. 'So, explain yourself, Bethany. What is it you're doing here and how do you know Quinn?'

With a heavy sigh, she told them the story of how she had come to meet Mr Quinn and how he had used his magic to let her come into the hotel. She described her meeting with Sir Stoames, her time in the kitchen, the giant, Maggie-Maggie and her suspicion that the ghosts and spirits were trapped in the hotel. 'I'm going to find the giant's tongue,' she said boldly. 'Maybe you can help me.'

The leprechauns listened patiently to her story. When she finished they convened in a tight circle, discussing what she had just told them. They had a vote then raised their hands unanimously.

Flannigan addressed Bethany. 'We put it to the vote and we've decided: it's only fair we let you go. Under normal circumstances we would do something really terrible to you, but on account of Quinn we're going to be lenient.'

'But I'm visible now!' Bethany protested. 'I thought you

were going to help me.'

'Help yourself is our rule. Honest, we would take you with us if you'd fit, but you're a little large for where we're going.'

'Well, where are you going?' she asked.

Flannigan pointed to a patch of wall with a hole in it, just like the one she had seen with Maggie-Maggie that she had taken for a mouse hole. Bethany would be lucky to fit her hand in, never mind her whole body.

'But you've got to help,' she pleaded. 'If I wander about the hotel like this I'm bound to be caught and I'll never get back to my parents. I already overheard Sir Stoames saying he wanted rid of me.' Her eyes welled up with tears.

The leprechauns exchanged uncomfortable glances. Seamus dodged out of the way of a falling teardrop. The four of them collected in a circle again and argued amongst themselves.

'But she knows Quinn.'

'She's not one of us.'

'Maybe she can lead us to some gold!'

'Shut up, Donovan.'

Eventually, the group broke apart and Flannigan stepped forward. 'Truth be told, young lady, we want out o' this place ourselves or at least break the spell that keeps us here. We'll help you as much as we can, on account of Quinn. He's a distant cousin of ours. A bit of a loner but a great sense of humour. And we always stick by family.'

Seamus, the bearded leprechaun, came forward and took another handful of dust from his pouch, blowing it on to Bethany. 'Yeartha don toory.'

Everything surrounding her started to grow. The ceiling stretched upwards, the walls spread apart. It was only when she looked to the floor and saw it shooting towards her that she realised her body was shrinking. It felt like taking a huge breath inwards and falling down at the same time. The leprechauns appeared to grow in size as she diminished, until she reached eye level with them. Their faces were even uglier up close – extremely large in relation to their bodies and stretched into mischievous grins.

'Right,' said Flannigan. His voice no longer sounded high-pitched but low and authoritative. 'We better be moving. Keep up and the ferrets won't get you.'

'Ferrets? What ferrets?'

The one they called Donovan giggled uncontrollably at her. He seemed younger than the others. 'She's so normal-sized now.'

Pat clipped him over the head with his hand. Flannigan was already leading the way. They all dutifully followed, moving in single file into the hole.

The tunnel was round and long and it was just like Bethany imagined entering a rabbit's burrow would be. A faint greenish glow illuminated the way, generated from jewels embedded in the wall at regular intervals. The passage led down to a fork, then carried on to a junction with several tunnels shooting off in different directions. The further down they went, the more twists and turns they had to negotiate. It made her dizzy trying to make sense of their zigzag journey, moving up and down and along and through. She imagined the tunnels permeated the entire hotel, dodging the golden threads and connecting with dozens of rooms.

They all moved very cautiously behind Flannigan, stopping when he stopped, listening when he listened. He must have been worried about the ferrets he mentioned as he was alert to the slightest sound. When he was sure the way ahead was safe, they all started sprinting until they had reached a wooden door. Flannigan banged on it impatiently and a hatch slid open. A set of eyes squinted at him suspiciously.

'Who's that?'

'It's me, Flannigan.'

'Oh, right you are. Did you find any gold, Flannigan?'

'Ah now, truth be told, we didn't find a crumb of it.'

'That's a crying shame, so it is.'

'A shame, to be sure,' agreed Flannigan. 'But we did manage to steal some fish from the kitchen.'

'Well,' said the man at the hatch, sighing with disappointment. 'I suppose you better come in.'

'If you wouldn't mind.'

Bolts and locks were undone and the door opened. All five of them traipsed in. If the tunnels resembled a warren then this was the burrow. Dozens of leprechauns moved about the cave-like interior. There was singing and movement and warmth. A dazzling glow of light nearly blinded Bethany as she came in from the darkness of the tunnel. There were piles of golden objects filling the place: golden rings, golden clocks, golden picture frames, golden coins and even several golden statues of leprechauns, all presumably stolen from the hotel.

The rest of the cave was a bright-green colour. Four-leaf clovers had grown over nearly every available space. Almost fifty leprechauns were moving purposefully around the area, some polishing gold, singing songs, drinking and dancing in rowdy groups. A dozen of them were involved in trying to write words in a blank book. For them it was the size of a double bed and they were attempting without much luck to guide a black pencil across its surface. An argument had developed between them as to who had caused the pencil to squiggle so much. Another group was practising magical tricks with the dust, creating miniature firework displays for each other, each performance causing them to brag and boast even louder, then take their turn to impress the others.

'What's this?' asked the extremely bearded leprechaun that had let them in. He looked Bethany up and down suspiciously whilst chewing on the nib of his pipe. Others sensed her strangeness and edged over to inspect her.

'Now I know what you're thinking, Flaherty,' said Flannigan defensively. 'But if you just hear me out I'm sure you'll see why we agreed to help her.'

'Help her?!' huffed the older leprechaun.

'Aye,' said Flannigan. 'Help her.'

Virtually all the leprechauns had stopped what they were doing now and congregated around Bethany. Their grinning faces brimmed with curiosity. They had never seen anything like her before. They muttered amongst themselves, excitedly at first, then with more agitation and hostility when they realised she was human. The nearest ones poked and prodded her to see if she was real.

Flannigan stood at the head of the crowd with his hands on his hips, shooshing them to be quiet. When they had eventually settled down he nodded at Bethany. 'Go on now. Tell them how you came to be here.'

Nervously, she shuffled forward, cleared her throat and told them how she had come to be a living ghost in the hotel. The leprechauns listened intently and broke into uproarious laughter at the mention of Mr Quinn and his mischievous antics. The sound of this high, infectious cackling made further patches of four-leaf clovers sprout up from the floor. By the time the story had reached its end there was a fresh blanket of green surrounding the group and the leprechauns were clutching their sides. They were clearly spirits that loved to see others get into trouble.

Flaherty was first to regain his composure. He sighed from the laughter as if he was someone that had just finished a satisfying meal. 'Ah, it's good to see Quinn is giving them a run for their money.'

Flannigan nodded his head sagely and addressed the whole room. 'So you see, if we help Bethany here, she might succeed where others have failed. Quinn has seen something unique in her that might help us break the curse o' this hotel. She is, after all, a living thing and the usual rules might not apply to her.'

'Why don't we let her lead us to the portal?' replied the older leprechaun. 'We could escape to the outside and finally be free of this place. We don't want to waste our time on some mad plan to find the giant's tongue.'

'You know as well as I do that door will be protected with all manner of curses, guards and spells. And why would Quinn come back if he didn't have to? It'll be jinxed in every way. No, I say we help the girl.'

Faces pondered and frowned but were less sure of this second option. By the sound of all the leprechauns murmuring, it seemed clear that they were not prepared to put their trust in a human.

Bethany tried to think of some way to sway their opinion. 'How long have you been here?' she asked in the loudest, most confident voice she could muster.

There was a pause in the debate as all eyes turned towards her.

'Too long!' shouted a leprechaun from the back.

'And was it because you couldn't pay your bill?' she said.

At the mention of the bill, there was widespread unrest. The crowd broke into a loud rabble of arguments. Some accused, some disputed the amount, some corrected the details, but all were in agreement that they had been tricked. It made the leprechauns angry and serious, and the sound of their shouting caused the four-leaf clovers to wither and die.

Eventually Flannigan shouted louder than anyone. 'Silence!' He turned to Bethany. 'That's why we've gone underground. That's why we've *had* to go underground. Stoames wanted us to pay off our bill with hard work and, if there's one thing we leprechauns pride ourselves on, it's our lack of hard work.'

There was a great cheer.

'I don't mind working hard,' said one voice.

'Shut up, Donovan. Furthermore, the crook we know only as the unnameable *J* stole our pots of gold. To steal a leprechaun's gold is the most terrible and unforgiveable crime there is and we will not rest until we find it and bring the culprit to justice.'

There was another cheer.

'You know, maybe we can help each other,' said Bethany with a flash of inspiration. She thought of the pots hidden away in Stoames's private vault. 'If you help me find the giant's tongue, I can tell you where your gold is hidden.'

A hundred eyes widened and glinted and each leprechaun echoed the word 'gold' as if they were lost in a dream.

'You better not be lying to us, girl,' Flaherty warned.

'I'm not. I promise,' Bethany reassured him. She described the pots and the way they had sparkled and glittered strangely.

Any doubt on the leprechauns' part disappeared. 'Well, we can't turn down a deal like that,' Flaherty admitted. He stroked his beard and gave a short nod of his head. 'We'll help you, girl.'

There was one last cheer and the group of leprechauns began muttering excitedly to one another about getting their gold back.

'But tell me, child, why do you want to find the giant's tongue?' Flaherty asked, fixing Bethany with a steely look.

Unsure of herself, she explained what she had seen in the kitchen and what Maggie-Maggie had mentioned about *J*'s name. 'The giant might be the only one powerful

131

enough to say *his* name, if I can help him speak. That's why the giant's tongue was taken in the first place. There's something about *his* name that he's trying to protect. I don't know what it is, but it must be powerful if he's stopping everyone from saying it.'

Bethany felt a little foolish, realising how her plan sounded, but much to her surprise, Flaherty was contemplating what she had said with a serious look on his face. 'It's an enchanted name, all right, protected by powerful forces. Four of our kind have tried to use their magic to reveal his full name. But each has suffered the consequences.'

The leprechauns went deathly quiet. Their grins dropped from their faces. Flaherty waved his pipe in the direction of the piles of golden objects. Four golden statues of leprechauns stood amongst the clutter. On closer inspection, their faces were frozen in expressions of horror. Whatever had happened to them had turned them suddenly into pure gold.

A moment of respectful silence followed as the leprechauns considered the fate of their companions. Heads bowed.

Flaherty broke the silence with an unexpected stamp of his foot. 'All right, now. Think! Where would you hide a giant's tongue?'

The crowd perked up at the question. They began shouting out suggestions.

'In a tongue-shaped box.'

'On top of a wardrobe.'

'Inside a large shoe.'

Bethany stepped forward. 'The cleaning ladies said that it was likely to be in an area of unusually high magical activity.'

'How about the starpool? That's magical.'

'There's always lots of tongues in the restaurant,' joked Seamus. 'And they must use a lot of magic for the menus.'

'Me, me,' cried Donovan, dancing on the spot. 'I know a place where there's lots of tongues and it's especially magical.'

Flannigan took a deep breath inwards. Bethany felt sure he was preparing to shout out a particularly loud 'Shut up, Donovan.' But before he could say it the freckle-faced youngster suggested, 'In the library.'

Flannigan pondered this. Flaherty, too, considered the suggestion. They both giggled.

'You know,' Flannigan said. 'That's the most useful thing you've ever said, Donovan.'

'Oh-oh, do I get a prize?' he asked excitedly.

'Yes. Yes, you do. Come here.'

Donovan eagerly ran over to Flannigan.

'Close your eyes.'

The young leprechaun closed his eyes.

Flannigan removed a sardine from his pouch that he must have stolen from the kitchen. It was as long as his arm. He took hold of its tail in both hands, swung it in a circle several times to gain momentum, then slapped Donovan solidly in the face with it, sending him crashing to the floor.

The crowd of leprechauns burst into manic, cackling

laughter and four-leaf clovers popped up everywhere.

Donovan opened his eyes, shook his head and beamed with a satisfied grin.

'It tasted a little bit of fish,' he remarked. 'But otherwise that was fine.'

This sent the others off into another bout of giggles.

Leprechauns, Bethany decided, were not entirely to be trusted.

CHAPTER ELEVEN

THE LIBRARY OF SINGING TONGUES

Pat, Seamus, Donovan and Flannigan volunteered to lead Bethany to the library. She didn't understand why a library would be a good place to find a tongue, but she was getting used to nothing making sense in the hotel. As they prepared to leave, she drew a diagram of Stoames's office and the exact place where his secret vault could be found. Flaherty memorised the tune that would unlock the door and the leprechauns danced excitedly at the prospect of retrieving their bills and gold.

'You know, I've always stayed away from humans but you're not so bad,' Flaherty admitted begrudgingly. 'Good luck to you, Bethany. And remember, whilst the spirit in control of this hotel may be incredibly powerful and almost certain to destroy you, never underestimate your own strength.'

'Um, right. Thanks.'

'Goodbye.'

He gave a formal little bow as Flannigan led the group back into the tunnel. The door closed on the scene of dozens of grinning leprechauns waving farewell. Bethany was soon running to keep up as Pat and Seamus sprinted off. They moved in silence, even Donovan contained himself, as if they were under the constant threat of being discovered.

Bethany stuck closely by Flannigan as he was the only one who seemed to have a clear idea of where he was going. With so many junctions and turns, the passages seemed as difficult and confusing to negotiate as the corridors of the hotel. They changed routes many times, doubling-back on themselves, carrying on in circles, reaching dead ends. She couldn't understand how the tunnels worked, since the hotel was constantly shifting about, and she guessed that they too had the ability to change.

'How on earth do you find your way around the hotel?' she whispered to Flannigan as he was trying to decide which direction to take at a crossroads.

'You have to use your instincts,' he told her quietly. 'Get to know the hotel. It's like being trapped in someone else's dream. Yes, that's it. Like someone else's dream. There are ways to move round it – things that are always there, even though they shift, and things that come as a surprise.'

'It's a mad place!' muttered Bethany.

'To be sure. But, you see, you're thinking of it in terms of a place. The hotel's a living thing. More than that, even. It's a spirit in itself. A powerful one. One that mesmerises other spirits. It changes and grows and presents itself differently to each one of us that looks at it, until it finds the exact thing we want. So when we leprechauns first came here all we saw was gold hidden everywhere, whereas a water spirit might see rivers and streams and waterfalls. That's why you might upset it all.'

'What do you mean?'

Flannigan scratched his chin. He'd stopped moving altogether. 'Because what you see isn't like what the rest of us see. Besides, there's something human about this place. Spirits have never wanted hotels before, or paid bills, or needed all sorts of activities to keep them busy. Those are human things. Some of the ghosts see that but are too scared to do anything. Some of us spirits are trying to fight it but don't understand it. You, though, you're a living human. That gives you strength against it.'

'I'm not strong,' Bethany said, blushing.

'Maybe you don't realise it, but let me tell you something. When you said you fed the giant and it stopped the hotel's power for a moment, it wasn't because of the cream bun. It was your act of kindness. That broke the spell and that's a rare gift. I think that's what Quinn sees in you.'

'I think Quinn brought me here because he thought it would be funny. All he seems to enjoy is getting me into trouble.'

'That's not entirely fair,' Flannigan said. 'Quinn's a spirit of mischief. He likes to play tricks on humans, true, but he is using his power for a deeper cause. All the tricks he has played on you have been a way of making you stronger whilst revealing the truth about this hotel. You see, Quinn has the uncanny knack of glimpsing the true nature of things, that's why he finds everything so funny. But he has seen pure goodness in you, Bethany, in the same way that he has seen pure evil at the heart of this hotel. Don't forget that. If you hope to help your —'

But Flannigan didn't get a chance to finish what he was about to say because a noise came rushing from the tunnel up ahead. It was the sound of something moving rapidly towards them and it caused Seamus to jump to attention and his face drain of colour. 'FERRET!'

Quickly, the leprechauns drew their swords, which were an assortment of pins and toothpicks they had customised into weapons. The rustling, snuffling noise of the approaching creature grew in volume. Seamus clutched at his pouch, trying quickly to undo the string so that he could reach inside for some of his magic powder.

The ferret spirit came at them in a blur of motion. Bethany caught a brief glimpse before she was knocked backwards. Its pointed face filled the tunnel. Two beady, mean eyes looked out from the mass of white fur. As it opened its mouth to bite them a dazzling glitter of light filled the tunnel. The teeth were made entirely from diamonds and shone in the murk like a priceless necklace. It had the desired effect, hypnotising everyone long enough for the ferret to get near enough to launch an attack.

'Run! Run!' cried Flannigan as he stood his ground and lunged at the creature with his sword. He caught it on the cheek and it squealed, hissed and backed away.

Pat pushed Bethany down the tunnel. She tumbled down with him, somersaulting over Donovan, and landed in a pile. She could hear the ferret snapping a second time. When she got to her feet and looked, it was struggling with something green in its jaws.

'Flannigan!' she shouted. But there was no reply.

Seamus managed to throw a handful of his powder and there was a flash of light and smoke. Metal bars appeared in the tunnel between himself and the ferret and it bared its diamond teeth. The green object dropped from its jaws and the ferret squirmed backwards to find another route.

Something moved in the dirt beside Seamus. A hand appeared, quickly joined by a body. Flannigan pulled himself up from the ground where he had fallen. He brushed himself down and shook his mop of red hair. He looked around at the others. 'That was my best hat!' he complained.

They all laughed nervously and hurried on. It would only be a matter of time before the ferret found another way to them and they had to move quickly. The encounter must have given Flannigan more focus as he led them on decisively. In what seemed like a few turns, they reached an opening that shone with bright light. They ran to the entrance, gathering by it, relieved and happy to have escaped the danger. Donovan made an expression at Bethany like he hadn't been afraid in the slightest, although he seemed to be shaking an awful lot.

'Now then,' Flannigan said. 'That's the library in there. You'll find all sorts of tongues. Big ones, small ones. Above all, we have to make sure we're not seen. Is everyone clear about that?'

Donovan's attention had drifted to a glint of coloured light by the entrance. 'Look,' he said excitedly. 'Gold!'

'Shut up, Donovan, I'm speaking,' Flannigan said instinctively. But when Bethany glanced across at the young leprechaun, he was reaching down to a single golden thread that stretched across the tunnel like a tripwire.

'No, Donovan. DON'T TOUCH IT!' she shouted.

It was too late. Donovan's hand had already reached for the thread and there was a crackling noise like a surge of electricity as he touched it. His face contorted with shock. His body froze in a pose that made him look like he was trying to run away. His features became still and turned a bright, lustrous yellow. Before their eyes, he transformed into a golden statue of himself. The strand quivered and fell like a loose hair, its power spent.

Not a single word was spoken for several minutes.

'Oh, Donovan,' Flannigan said eventually.

They all bowed their heads.

Pat sighed. 'It's the way he would have wanted to go.'

'And he makes a nice bit of gold, so he does,' added Scamus.

Flannigan's mood lifted. 'Right enough, that *is* a nice bit of gold.'

The three remaining leprechauns jumped on to the statue and had quickly tied their belts round it so they could drag it back to their den. Their eyes were filled with obvious glee.

'It'd be a crime to just leave him here,' Flannigan said when he caught Bethany glowering at him. He reluctantly pulled himself away from Donovan's statue and shook his head. 'We'll have to leave you here, I'm afraid. We'll try and make it back but . . . well, we're not having a good time of it. There is bad luck at every turn. We would be fools to keep courting it.'

'But how will I find the giant's tongue on my own?' asked Bethany.

'Look,' said Flannigan. He led her out of the tunnel and she was confronted with a wall of noise. It was like hundreds of people talking at her simultaneously in such a loud and cacophonous babble that it was impossible to make sense of a single voice. She clutched at her ears to try and drown out the noise as Flannigan showed her the contents of the library.

Rows of shelves stretched before them, tall as skyscrapers. They were not packed with books, though. Instead, there were hundreds of strangely shaped glass jars, each one containing a wriggling eel. Although as soon as Bethany looked closer, she realised that they weren't eels inside the jars but tongues! Hundreds and thousands of tongues all flapping away excitedly.

'Oh,' she said.

'If you find it anywhere, it's most likely to be here. Best place to hide a tongue is amongst lots of tongues, as the old leprechaun saying goes.'

She could hardly take in the bizarre sight. The jars rattled on their shelves with the force of the tongues. 'What are they doing?' she wondered out loud, having to raise her voice to be heard over the din.

'Telling stories,' Flannigan shouted back. 'What else?'

'Right. Of course. How stupid of me.' She chewed her lip. The nearest jars were as big as houses. It would be a formidable task to get even one of them opened, never mind searching through hundreds of them. 'How am I going to reach them?'

Flannigan looked her up and down and compared her to the gargantuan stacks of shelves. 'Ah, you've got a point there. Seamus, come over here a second.'

He ran over.

'She needs to be back to her normal size.'

'Maybe we could all work together?' Bethany suggested hopefully. She realised how exposed she would be if she were bigger and she didn't want to be left on her own. 'You know, a sort of group effort.'

The leprechauns were keen to get back to their den, though. The dust fizzled in the air and tickled as Seamus recited the words. Everything shrank. Flannigan and Seamus disappeared. Bethany felt a sickening rush upwards. It was as if all the size was being squashed out of the room and transferred to her body. For a moment, she realised how the giant must feel – immense. Then she remembered this was her normal size.

She leaned down to the leprechauns. They looked much funnier from up high and their voices sounded high and squeaky again.

'We'll have to leave you now. Good luck,' said Flannigan.

'Goodbye,' said Pat and Seamus.

Bethany waved at them as they disappeared into the hole with their treasure. She felt quite glum that they had to leave her here, and her heart fluttered with relief as Seamus returned. He untied his pouch of dust from his belt and offered it up to her. She had to crouch down on the floor to hear him.

'I shouldn't be doing this and there's not much left,' he told her. 'But you better take it. It might help you if you need to get small or big again. Just remember that to make yourself small you say the words "Yeartha don toory". But to make yourself big you say "Yeartha don toory". *Don't*, on any account, get the two confused.'

'But . . .?'

There was a call from the tunnel. 'I'd better go,' Seamus said. 'Here.' He pushed the pouch between her fingertips and ran off, laughing a lunatic laugh.

'Thanks,' said Bethany. She carefully placed the pouch into the pocket of her spirit jeans and stood up. She felt incredibly tall even though she was still half the height of the shelves around her. It quickly became apparent that this was the sort of library where it would be difficult to draw attention to yourself, though.

She walked to the end of the aisle and found herself standing in a grand, circular room, domed like the interior of a cathedral. The rows of shelves were arranged alphabetically in a circle from *A* to *Z*, each section jutting out from the walls like spokes from a wheel. At the centre of the auditorium was a hub of curtained cubicles. Each was attached with a hooded funnel and spirits were entering them with their jars.

Inside, some strange process was at work. The booths rocked with weird noises. Sparks of coloured lights flashed from underneath the curtain as if fireworks were being set off.

Bethany pretended to be browsing one of the many shelves as a spirit brushed past her. A plant with bright pink flowers floated through the air, using its dangling roots to propel itself forward like a jellyfish. It moved towards a booth without giving her a moment's notice.

There were so many jars with tongues that it was hard to know where to begin. The shape of the jars differed as greatly as their contents. There were ones as big as church bells, ones with flat heads like anvils, ones as round as goldfish bowls, ones that were droopy like melted candles. There was every shape imaginable. There were Greek urns, flowerheads, teardrops, bottles, beaks, stalagmites, trunks, horns and shells. There were ones shaped into strange creatures, clawed hands, winged dogs, snarling Chinese dragons. It looked like a collection of immaculately crafted ice sculptures.

The contents were no less striking. There were tongues as sharp as swords, stubby tongues that wriggled with gossip, fat tongues that flattered, tongues that had blackened from telling curses. And each flickered inside its jar like a single flame.

The giant's tongue could easily be hidden among such a collection. Bethany's first instinct was to look for the biggest but realised that would be too obvious. It could have been shrunk, as she had been, making it much easier to conceal.

She read out the inscriptions on the jars. *History of*

Abominable Demons, History of Invisible Portals, History of Imps. Further up the *H* aisle was *How to Manifest in Physical Form, How to Manipulate and Control Humans, How to Shape Time.*

She sighed. It was all very confusing and overwhelming.

She tried humming her favourite tune and thinking of her favourite colour – she remembered Stoames telling her that this might help. But before she could decide if she preferred orange to green, she thought of an idea. She went to the middle of the aisle and searched the shelf. Her finger hovered over the titles. *Hidden Realms, Hideous Forms, Hiding Spirits.* She reached an empty space where a jar had been removed, but as her finger moved past it she touched something solid. An inscription briefly appeared: *Hiding, A How To Guide.*

'Perfect!' she muttered.

She tucked the jar under her arm and made her way towards the booths. She waited for a small white snow spirit to pass by before she sneaked into one of the cubicles. She quickly drew the curtain so that no one would see her. The interior was no bigger than a changing room and looked bare except for a simple wooden stool. There was a pipe releasing a fine mist into the top half of the booth and a funnel was gradually pulling up any excess vapour.

Bethany took a seat and unscrewed the jar. As soon as the lid came off, the tongue shot into the air, swimming fish-like into the vapour. A phantom mouth appeared around it.

'Hiding,' it announced. The word appeared in the vapour

in large green letters. The title shimmered and revolved in the air to reveal all sorts of things hidden behind it. Lizards and secret doorways and camouflaged creatures all appeared briefly before they were sucked up the funnel.

The tongue started to vibrate rapidly, producing a strange yodelling babble of noise. It was such a shocking, unpleasant sound that Bethany jumped up from her chair and was about to run out of the cubicle, thinking she had caused another disaster. But as she looked up she saw that the noises were causing images to appear in the mist above her. The vapour was somehow converting the sounds into images.

The picture of a room emerged from the mist, although it wasn't like watching the picture on a television. This picture appeared in three dimensions as if it was a semi-transparent model. It showed an old-fashioned room with an armchair, a grandfather clock and an open fire. Then it began to reveal good places to hide. It must have been meant for spirits, though, as all the places were very strange, like inside a mirror, or an extra shadow of the armchair, or disguised as a flame in the fire.

The tongue changed to flirruping, stuttering noises. This made the image of the room disperse in smoky wisps. It was replaced with scenes of wind spirits hiding themselves as clouds, gnomes turning themselves into stones, a giant disguising itself as a mountain.

Then the noises started to describe hidden objects. Much to Bethany's delight, the first one was a leprechaun's pot of gold. This was placed into a hole a foot off the ground like an invisible cupboard. Next came a goat man's set of musical pipes that were hidden as hollow reeds on mountain rocks. All sorts of examples flashed up in the image-vapour but nothing resembling a giant's tongue. Gradually, the images became fainter and more confused as the tongue ran out of energy. She grabbed hold of the jar and scooped the tongue out of the vapour. It felt like handling a particularly large and unpleasant slug and she dropped it back in the jar as quickly as possible before she squealed. She screwed the lid back on, slinked out of the booth and returned it to the shelf.

She had another idea that might help her. She carefully snuck along to the Q section. Maybe the library had some information on Quinn that might help her find him since he was so elusive. Her eyes scanned along the *Qs*. *Qualified Spirit Doctors, Quarrelsome Spirits*. She stopped at a gap. There on the shelf was Mr Quinn himself, standing half a foot tall, holding himself very still as if he was pretending to be one of the jars. Bethany poked her face at him. He quivered and his grin twitched.

'That's not very funny,' she said. 'Or realistic.'

He looked up at her and tittered.

'Stoames has sent your shadow after you. You're in a lot of trouble.'

Quinn somersaulted off the shelf and landed on the ground. He moved away from her, making long gliding motions on the floor as if he was ice-skating across the polished surface.

'I'm not doing it. I'm not following you,' Bethany said. She folded her arms and refused to move. But Quinn skated round her, pirouetting and making funny little jumps. It was like watching a very fat ballet dancer and she couldn't help laughing. Reluctantly, she let him lead her back to the *H* section.

He found the spot he was looking for and clicked his fingers at the shelves. A glass jar rattled and pushed itself into view. It was shaped like a stag's head and it was very dusty as if no one had bothered to look at it before. The label read, *History of Stagtree Knoll*. The tongue inside limped weakly. 'Is this it? Is this the giant's tongue?' Bethany asked hopefully.

Quinn shook his head. No.

'This better not be a trick,' she warned him and she lifted the jar off the shelf. 'You'll probably not be here when I get back so I'll just say . . .'

She didn't know what it was she wanted to say to him.

'Be careful,' she finally decided.

He nodded his head in acknowledgement. She scurried across to the booths, narrowly avoiding a wind spirit that whirled by in a miniature tornado.

Bethany drew the curtain and released the tongue. It moved sluggishly at first, then leaped into the air as if it had just come awake.

'Oh, um, yes. Yes, that's right,' it said. 'The History of Stagtree Knoll.'

CHAPTER TWELVE

THE HISTORY OF STAGTREE KNOLL

As before, the words appeared in the image-vapour, this time in colours of peacock-blue and mushroom-grey. The tongue started to make its cacophony of sounds, braying and clacking and squawking, until a shape began to form. A bird's-eye view of Stagtree Knoll appeared. It showed the village as it was now, and Bethany recognised the factory and the park with the rusted roundabout and the street with her house on. It was the first normal thing she had seen since she had been in the hotel and it made her want to be back home, tucked up safely in bed.

But the peaceful scene of her village was quickly disturbed. Time reversed, like a film running backwards, so that newer houses disappeared, telephone lines vanished, electricity pylons dismantled themselves. Woodland began to claim back the patchwork of fields. Hundreds of years passed, until the forest had spread and prospered and all that was left of the village was the original Stoames mansion and several small huts with thatched roofs.

The mansion reverted back to its original incarnation as a castle. The stones used to build it were a bright shade with sharp edges not yet smoothed away by wind and rain. It was large but not particularly impressive. In fact, it seemed quite basic, nothing more than a square building with turrets at each corner, although situated in large grounds with busy stables.

The babbling sound of the tongue changed pitch and blooms of green filled the cubicle. It showed the forest and its abundant wildlife. Deer grazed under the shade of the plush trees, alert for a moment as a flock of birds swirled overhead. A wild pig snuffled in the undergrowth. Squirrels frolicked across branches. Bethany could hardly believe it was the same place as the drab, boring village she was used to.

But an even bigger revelation was the spirit world. It appeared as a second landscape, superimposed over the physical landscape of the forest. It seemed to be made up of areas of bright and dark energy, and was populated with strange creatures like those Bethany had seen in the hotel, moving through the scene in subtle bodies of light and shade. And it was every bit as fertile and lively as the forest.

Water nymphs played in the river, their fluid bodies drifting into the shapes of strong currents and otters and darting salmon. Bird spirits glided through the air, catching the forms of each bird that spread its wings. There were even ghosts that hovered over marshland at the edge of the forest. Bethany could finally see how spirits existed. The two worlds joined at lots of little points, one influencing the other. And if enough energy built up around something, like a plant or animal, a spirit with those characteristics would grow. Spirits were bundles of energy and the forest was alive with them.

The largest, a tree spirit, was an immense, gangly form that wandered through the forest like a farmer checking his crops. It occasionally stopped to assume the form of a particular tree and it gave that plant an unusual surge of energy before it moved on. Almost every animal and vegetable spirit stopped to speak to it. There were even earth spirits that bore a striking resemblance to the gnomes Mr Quinn had lined up outside the butcher's shop. Their bright clothing was made up from toadstool skins that they had draped over their podgy bodies and they crawled about the roots of the tree spirit like a group of ladybirds gently grooming the frayed ends.

The tree spirit immersed itself into a giant oak tree that stood on top of a knoll. It must have been a comfortable form as it settled into it effortlessly and the tree began to surge and sparkle with energy. It made Bethany think of someone dressing in their favourite clothes.

Her attention shifted to the brightest being. This one danced and weaved through the forest in a dazzling point of light. It flitted across streams, down hillsides, through forest glades. The image vapour grew brighter as it focused on the origin of this energy. A stag appeared. It moved gracefully into a glade. The other animals and spirits sensed its power immediately and its presence seemed to have a calming effect on them.

This was no ordinary stag. It was a rare beast. Elegant. Majestic. A form that had distilled some pure animal essence, causing a powerful spirit to bond with it. The stag shone with light. Whilst describing the creature, the tongue shifted into a smooth, melodic singing. It gave Bethany a warm sensation throughout her body, a feeling that she was seeing something so unique and wonderful that she dared not take her eyes off it for a second. But the image vapour shifted and returned to the castle.

The grounds were bustling with activity. A group of lords were being helped on to horseback. Servants passed them long bows and quivers full of arrows. Their tunics and strange haircuts made them look medieval, although Bethany couldn't be sure as she had never concentrated much on history. Now she wished she had.

One lord stood out from the others. He was dressed in grand clothes and, by the way the others fussed over him, he must have owned the castle. There was something determined and powerful in his manner and he was physically striking, even though he was younger than anyone else. He boasted a head of fine blond hair and stark blue eyes. An even stranger aspect to him, though, was the black shape that flittered above his shoulder in the spirit realm. It seemed to react to his show of power as he commanded those around him. *Is it a bad spirit?* Bethany wondered. *A demon?* It was definitely draining others of their energy, feeding off the natural glow that all living things seemed to possess and turning it into a dull fog. It grew and flickered like a black flame, taking light instead of giving it.

The group of hunters cheered as the blond-haired lord led them out of the gates and into the surrounding forest. The effect on the woods was like a large boulder dropped into water. Wildlife scattered. The lord led the riders as they caught sight of a pack of deer. The animals bolted in every possible direction, racing to avoid the shower of arrows as the humans charged them.

Bethany had an inkling of what was coming and didn't want to look. She knew that the lord would catch a glimpse of the stag of light and that he would immediately recognise the power of the animal. Bethany had to watch as the stag lifted its head and its eyes locked for the briefest moment with the hunter's gaze. Instinctively, it ran, leaping so power-fully that it almost escaped in that first precious encounter.

Almost. The black flame exerted its influence on the blond-haired lord. It gave him the instinct to ride his horse in the right direction and he caught another glimpse of the stag's antlers moving before they were lost in a mass of branches. He charged after it blindly, galloping into the thickest part of the forest. He guided his horse under low trees, up muddy hillocks and across the crumbling banks of the river. He pushed onwards harder and harder but he only succeeded in catching another tantalising glance of his prey as it turned away from him. It made its capture even more desirable.

As quick and agile as the stag was, it could not throw off its pursuer and it was sensing the danger. It moved down into a valley and led the hunter into a mass of brambles, hoping to entangle him. The dense undergrowth slowed the lord down but he was an expert rider and he forced his horse on regardless. A wild greed was now guiding him past the point any other hunter might have stopped. The demon moved above his shoulder like a flag caught in wind, rippling with excitement.

The stag moved up the other side of the valley whilst its pursuer struggled to find a clear route. Then, with the briefest turn of his head, the lord caught a much closer glimpse of his prey. He turned his horse, spurred it hard, and cleared a wall of thorny vines.

The chase attracted the attention of the spirits of the forest. They sensed a deep significance in the hunt. To them, it was much clearer how unique the deer was and how much of a threat the lord was becoming. They tried to intervene. Low branches swung and tried to knock him off his horse. Stones rolled out of nowhere, upsetting his steed's footing. Storm clouds filled the sky, dark and ominous, and blasted him in gales and rain. But his willpower overcame each obstruction as if he understood all too well the invisible spirit world around him and knowing that he held the true power in the physical world. He rode on through exhaustion, through defeat, an insatiable desire urging him on.

The stag of light, in turn, never gave up for a moment. It leaped across streams, bounded over rocky crevices, vaulted through marshland. Even as the sky darkened and thunder erupted in terrifying rumbles, it moved as effortlessly as if it was involved in a playful game. And, as it came to a fork in the path, it managed to lose its pursuer as it ran one way and the blond-haired lord galloped the other. Finally, it seemed, it was free.

Deep down, though, Bethany knew that the hunt could not end well. Riddled with apprehension, she watched the stag burst through a wall of trees and stop suddenly. It was confused at what it saw. The chase had brought the creature in a huge circle back to the castle.

The stag hesitated, turned left quickly and ran up the knoll with the oak tree on top of it so it could judge which route it could safely take. The gangly tree spirit, merged with the oak, swayed its branches in an effort to warn the stag, but it was too late. A flash of gold shot out from the bushes.

The stag's proud head lifted, glimpsed the spark of colour and flinched as the golden arrow whistled through the air and connected with its forehead. It hit with such force that it pinned the deer to the trunk of the oak tree. Its body shuddered and its hooves churned the ground helplessly, as if it was still trying to escape.

The blond-haired lord appeared from the bushes, lowering his bow. He dismounted his horse and ran over to the slain beast. He looked half-crazed, his bedraggled hair falling in a tangled mop over his face, his mouth caught in a crooked snarl of victory. The demon on his shoulder tripled in size.

The furious reaction of the spirit world matched the ferocity of the rising storm. Spirits of all kinds swarmed around the knoll and the dead body of the stag. The blond-haired lord must have sensed something important was happening around him, as he paused before he kneeled down by his prize. His hand reached for the golden arrow. At that moment there was a curious configuration of spirits. The tree spirit was immersed in the oak tree; the deer spirit hung over the slain stag, and the demon hovered beside the lord's shoulder. A flash of lightning burst from the storm clouds above them and struck the tree. There was a moment of intense bright light and a great blast of energy that seemed to shake both the spiritual and physical realms. The individual spirits of the tree, the stag and the demon flickered and disappeared. Something luminous and powerful entered the lord's body.

The lightning strike hurled him away from where he stood and he landed on the ground in a smouldering heap. Fellow hunters and servants came running from the castle, brought by the tremendous blast of lightning, afraid but curious. A group gathered by the gates, staring at the shocking sight of the knoll, the scorched oak tree and the stag. Most of all, they stared at the collapsed figure of their master.

Only the most loyal servant was brave enough to approach. He edged closer cautiously, sensing something strange and terrible had happened. The others watched him with horrible fascination. The omens of the stag and tree were bleak and the lord should by all natural laws be dead, but his corpse began to twitch and move on the ground. The servant ran to him, grabbed him tightly by the shoulders and heaved him back to the safety of the castle to try to save him. Others reluctantly helped when they reached the gates.

But Bethany was too shocked to notice what happened next as she recognised the face of the servant. There, caught in the image vapour, were the unmistakable features of Sir Stoames. He was a younger man and looked humble in his modest clothing, but his upturned nose was there with tufts of unpleasant black hair peeking out.

The scene next showed the lord recovering in his castle, but something curious had happened to him. Whilst his body was unconscious in bed being faithfully nursed by Stoames, his spirit was transforming. A golden form was growing out of him, partly tree, partly stag, partly demon, as if these three spirits had fused with his own. Whatever it was, it was exerting a powerful force over the spirit realm. Ghosts came first and Bethany guessed these were the weakest inhabitants of the spirit world. They were drawn to this new entity like metal attracted to a magnet.

The force grew out of the lord's body in strands of gold. They were like the shoots of a plant but they moved towards the light of the ghosts, spreading and expanding in erupting bundles as they drained energy from them. And soon the spirits of the woodland were being pulled towards it to nourish it further.

The force thrived and grew among the foundations of the castle, altering the very substance of the building until it seemed like a living thing, dividing and organising itself. The spirit hotel appeared and more and more spirits were caught up in the luminous tangles. And all the while Sir Stoames tended to it, keeping away any threats from the physical world.

The tongue managed one last sequence of phrases to describe the giant emerging from a nearby mountain. It seemed as if the disturbance had stirred him, as if it could sense the strangeness of this new demon-human-spirit hybrid. He was a magnificent tower of light that formed into the arms, legs and face of the giant now trapped in the pit.

He strode boldly to the castle and grabbed at the freakish occupant. His hands ripped at the sprouting form like a man ripping out weeds from a garden. He had underestimated the power of the golden strands, though. They collected into strong tentacles that attacked the giant from every angle, tangling his arms and wrapping round his legs. They were swift and decisive and ruthless. The giant was dragged to the ground in seconds. He opened his mouth to speak, to say the name of this strange spirit, but golden creepers rushed around his face. Bethany looked away, knowing all too well what happened next.

The image vapour became fuzzy and vague. It showed how massive and powerful the spirit lord became by using the giant's energy to boost its own. It was now able to bridge the physical and spiritual realms. And it gave Stoames the first benefits of this new power. It separated him from his body, turning him into a ghost but fixing a transmigration patch to his corpse so that he could wear it like a costume in the physical realm. He soon found other bodies for the hotel so that they could be adapted for the spirits to dress up in.

The tours were just another activity to attract the spirits.

She could see that there was something cunning to the hotel in the way that it drew them into it, hypnotising them with its activities and displays of magic, whilst stealthily drawing its energy from them. It didn't keep all the spirits trapped but let a portion of them free to come and go so that they would return with more spirits, making it appear harmless. Other guests were less lucky, though, as Bethany had witnessed in the hall of bathtubs. They were having their magical energies extracted to fuel the hotel's growth, while the ghosts were being forced to help with the whole process.

The last few pictures in the image vapour showed the hotel expanding at an enormous rate and she couldn't help wondering when or if it would ever stop. It chilled her to the core, imagining how many spirits, ghosts and people could fall under its spell.

Bethany returned the singing tongue to its jar and closed the lid. For a moment, she sat where she was and tried to digest all the information she had seen. *Flannigan was right when he said there was something human about the hotel*, thought Bethany. *And if it is human, it means it has human weaknesses.*

She felt a renewed sense of purpose as she crept out of the cubicle and back along to the *H* section. Mr Quinn was waiting patiently on the shelf, swinging his legs. He stood up as she approached.

'You waited,' she said, pleasantly surprised.

Quinn smiled.

'So this is how he got his power?'

He smiled and nodded at her.

'And he's drawing all his power from the guests he attracts?'

Again, he smiled and nodded, nodded and smiled.

'But we still need to find the giant's tongue if we're going to stop him.'

He gave Bethany a proud, knowing grin and clicked his fingers. A gold embossed card appeared by his side, almost as tall as Quinn, and he held it like he was holding a door open for Bethany. She had to turn her head sideways to make out the picture of a golden tongue on the surface. 'What is that?' she asked.

Quinn looked very pleased with himself. He motioned at the card and seemed to be about to reveal its meaning when a worried look crossed his face. His smile faltered as his gaze drifted to the floor behind Bethany. He dropped the card and began jumping up and down on the shelf, pointing urgently at a shape moving towards them.

Bethany turned in that direction and for a moment didn't notice anything unusual. After all, she was used to seeing her shadow and, under normal circumstances, it wasn't something to be afraid of.

CHAPTER THIRTEEN

CARRIED AWAY

The first unusual thing about her shadow was how dark it had become. It made it appear ominous and strong, which is exactly what it was. The other strange thing was how quickly it could move. Before she had even blinked it flitted down the aisle and reattached itself to her feet. This didn't seem so bad, until it began to move. It tugged her so violently that she dropped the stag's head jar and it smashed impressively on the floor. The tongue wriggled like a goldfish that had leaped out of its bowl. Bethany leaned down to scoop it up, but her shadow walked her down the aisle before she had a chance.

'Stop that!' she shouted. 'What are you doing? You're supposed to be on my side, stupid!'

It was no good. She remembered what Sir Stoames had said about the shadows, that they were jinxed to obey the hotel. And there was nothing she could do to persuade hers

161

otherwise. Whatever dark magic had been used, the shadow was much stronger than her phantom body and it pulled at her with the intention of marching her out of the library. Bethany grabbed the nearest thing to her – the edge of a shelf – and held on as tightly as she could.

'Quinn. Help me! It's too strong.'

Quinn was running back and forth, peering over the ledge with mounting concern as his own shadow snaked up the bookshelves towards him. He looked as unsure of an escape route as Bethany was.

There was a powerful yank from her feet that nearly made Bethany fall flat on her face and her hands gripped the shelf even tighter. If her shadow was under the control of the hotel that meant it would lead her straight back to Stoames. It had gone beyond just being trapped here, she knew. She could end up like one of the guests in the bathtubs slowly having their spirits drained, while her physical body would end up being used as a costume by strange spirits wanting to go on a tour.

'QUINN!'

Her shadow heaved again. The bookshelf teetered, over-balanced and came crashing down on to the ground. Jars exploded on impact with the floor. A noise like a fallen chandelier halted the entire library. The scattered tongues began to babble in a rising chorus. Every spirit turned to see what was going on.

Bethany's shadow reacted quickly, pooling underneath her and dragging her along the floor. As soon as she realised what was happening, she started to scream, then grabbed the leg of an onlooker. A bird spirit squawked at her and it distracted Bethany's shadow long enough for her to get back on to her feet. She managed to make it several feet in the opposite direction before being whirled round and jerked back towards the exit, colliding with one of the cubicles. Image vapour hissed from a break in the pipe.

Over by the aisle, Quinn was being dragged backwards along the floor by his shadow. His hands scrabbled frantically for something to anchor himself to but he was having no luck.

Inspiration flashed across Bethany's mind. As she was manoeuvred around the cubicles, she crouched down, managed to hold herself still for a moment, then sprang into a high leap so that she had no contact with the floor. It made her shadow lose its grip and it went flying forwards as if it had been pulling a rope that had abruptly been let go. Bethany jumped towards Quinn. On the fourth leap her shadow caught up with her and swiped her feet from under her. She crashed into another cubicle. A second pipe cracked and sprayed its contents. The babbling tongues from the smashed jars were causing a swirling mess of pictures to appear in the leaking vapour. Her own voice broke outwards in a wavy red line. 'Quinn! Try jumping. It can't get you whilst you're in the air.'

She managed to leap free from her shadow's grip and continued to bounce across to the shelves, causing the top of her head to break through into the mist. Each glimpse revealed a battlefield of pictures: butterflies transforming into flapping books, unicorns making a racecourse from haunted woods.

The weirdness of the pictures caught her off guard and her shadow managed to knock her back to the ground, where it had the advantage. Mr Quinn was now bouncing several feet into the air and his arms flapped quickly as if he was attempting to take off. It looked so ridiculous that Bethany nearly burst into laughter, momentarily distracted from the seriousness of their situation. Her shadow darkened beneath her and carried her off towards the library's wide doorway.

As she glided by a shelf, Bethany reached her hand out, pulling it backwards as hard as she could. She watched as jars spilled across the floor. Even more clacking, gibbering, rasping tongues joined the cacophony. The mist was filling the library and it sparked and glowed as if a firework display was being launched in thick fog, and now golden strands peeled from the walls and began slashing and flicking restlessly through the cloud.

Bethany felt panicky and helpless. Her eyes scanned the chaos. Quinn appeared, somersaulting over some of the broken jars, but he was looking confused at which way to go, as hotel staff were gathering around the only exit.

'Go to the *H* section. There's a leprechaun hole,' Bethany shouted over to him. She tried to get to her feet again but it seemed as if she was getting weaker. Her arms and legs felt heavy. Her shadow pulled her towards the door, steering her away from anything she might latch on to.

She looked back for some support but Quinn had disappeared behind the fallen shelves. Her stomach lurched.

He wasn't leaping any more. 'Quinn?'

Spirits thronged together by the library entrance and they moved back to make a path for Bethany, staring at her with a mixture of fear and curiosity. Just as she was being dragged the last few feet to the doorway, she caught a flicker of motion along the floor. She saw a tiny body moving through the fog.

'Quinn?' she called out desperately.

'The next best thing,' Flannigan shouted back, sprinting towards her. He held a matchstick in his hand. Using it like a high jumper with a pole, he launched himself over the fallen shelves. The match head struck and ignited and he threw the flaming stick at the shadow. It landed on the shadow's arm, breaking its shape and making it flit across the floor. Pat and Seamus ran alongside Flannigan and launched their matchsticks. Her shadow moved quickly, as if stung by the flames, trying to reform itself.

'Light is the only way to deal with this sort of dark magic,' Flannigan said. 'Run, girl! We'll try and slow it down at least.'

Bethany didn't waste any time. She pulled herself off the floor and hurried towards the *H* section. She scanned the area for Quinn but couldn't spot him. Instead, amongst the piles of broken jars she saw a glint of light reflecting off the gold embossed card that he had dropped. She grabbed it and ran off up the aisle, only to notice a shadow racing past her, back towards the exit. Quinn's body was rigid as it rushed by, completely under the control of his shadow.

'NO!' she shouted. She tried to chase it but it was too

quick. She felt her heart sink as Quinn disappeared through the library doors and up a long corridor. She had no idea what to do without him. If he couldn't fight his way out with all his magic, how on earth could she expect to escape?

Bethany's thoughts raced. The leprechauns were having some success at herding her own shadow but they only had a few matches left. It was only a matter of time before it retrieved her for Stoames. She couldn't stay in the library for much longer, either – golden threads were snaking across the floor. She didn't know where to go or what to do.

Through the noise of all the tongues babbling, she recognised a familiar sound. A gurgling laugh. She peered down as the mists parted and a plump rat with a pink quiff of hair on its head grinned up at her.

'Quinn, is that you? But how did you . . .?'

The leprechauns shouted from the doorway. Her shadow had made it past them. Flannigan's faint voice called over to them. 'Run, girl! It's coming for you.'

She looked nervously to Quinn. His pink rat nose twitched and he blinked his eyes at her three times. A large object suddenly grew upwards from the ground. Bethany turned, took a step back and shrieked involuntarily. An exact copy of herself appeared at her side. The doppelgänger had an idiotic painted grin on its face.

Next, a tingling sensation spread across her body. Her ears itched and glowed with heat and sprouted from her head. She felt her nose stretching and pulling the rest of her face forward. A tail grew from the bottom of her spine and both feet drew back into themselves. For a horrible moment she expected to shrink in size and become a rat, but thankfully Quinn had spared her that particular fate.

Her shadow appeared and hesitated as it reached Bethany and her doppelgänger. For a moment, it couldn't decide which one to go for. It moved back and forth until it found itself comfortably fitting to the shape of the doppelgänger. Dutifully, it dragged it off.

Quinn the Rat winked at her. The relief was short-lived, however. The golden strands were violently slashing through the image vapour in an effort to control the outbreak of chaotic images. Bethany still had the card in her hand and tried to alert Quinn by waving it at him but he was already scuttling away. He wasn't the only one. Pat, Seamus and Flannigan ran back towards their hole as the library collapsed around them.

'Plan B!' Flannigan shouted, as he disappeared into the mists. 'Every leprechaun for himself!'

The spirits stared with concern at the smoke billowing out of the doors. Stoames had made it to the head of the crowd and was trying to reassure them. 'Please. Everything is fine,' he said, holding his hands up in a calming gesture. 'There's nothing to see here.'

Except there was a lot to see there, as all sorts of images slithered and shuffled and scampered in a riot of colour behind his back.

Quinn picked his moment well and scurried past Stoames into the crowd of spirits as a dispute rose over the danger of the fumes pouring out of the library. Bethany was far more conspicuous but she didn't want to be left behind, so she ducked her head low and quickly followed after him. Her transformed feet clopped noisily on the floor and she stumbled when she tried to run past Stoames, inadvertently barging into him. Luckily, she was barely noticed in all the confusion. Whatever she had been transformed into was strange enough to fool the other guests. Quinn had somehow made her body glow with the unusual energy that marked the spirits out from the ghosts and Bethany managed to join the crowd of guests without attracting too much attention.

Weird, grotesque faces frowned at her. A bear spirit growled down at her for treading on its paw. A giant swan clucked at her for interrupting its view. There was so much activity in the packed corridor that it was hard to see which way Quinn had gone and even harder trying to keep up with him as he threaded between feet.

'No need to push so hard!' complained a dark, ghoulish figure.

'I can't see anything with you in the way,' tutted a cricket.

Bethany kept her head down low and barged forwards despite the complaints. By the time she made it through the crowd, Quinn was a tiny dot disappearing through a doorway at the far end of the corridor. She followed him through the door and found herself standing in the hotel lobby she had first entered. It bustled with guests and staff and activity, looking as if it had doubled in size since she had last been there.

She clutched the card tightly in her hand and forced

herself into the centre of the foyer. With so much going on, it was impossible to tell which way Quinn had gone. She looked over at the front desk and noticed an argument erupting between one of the guests and a ghost attendant.

'But that's outrageous!' the spirit complained.

'I'm sorry, Sir, but the bill is correct,' the ghost explained. He held the list of outstanding items in his hand. 'You will have to discuss a method of payment with the management. We accept all forms of magic.'

The spirit, whom Bethany now recognised as the walrus-like creature she had seen in the cloakroom, was marched off by his own shadow. He began to harrumph and protest. She felt like saying something to make other guests aware of what was happening in front of them, but at that moment she noticed a rat scurrying up one of the spiral staircases and she bolted across the lobby.

She took the stairs two at a time. When she reached the first landing, she looked left and right but couldn't see a thing. Two gargoyles sat on the balcony, gossiping and clucking at the busy scene below them. They glared at Bethany with complete disdain.

She felt desperate and confused. *Where was Quinn going?* She turned the card over in her hand. There was a picture of a golden tongue on one side and the hotel slogan on the other, with the words 'admits two' written in smaller letters below it. But there was nothing else to indicate what it was for or any clue as to where she should go to use it.

An involuntary noise burst from her throat. She had meant to shout Quinn's name as loudly as she could, but what came out instead was a braying, hee-hawing sound.

With utter clarity, Bethany realised that she had been partially turned into a donkey. She thought of the grey, scruffy, slightly-stupid looking animals she had once seen at a petting zoo and felt uncontrollable anger. *This isn't fair! A donkey? Of all the things he could turn me into!* The gargoyles sneered at her. If she could have blushed, she would have. She hung her head in shame.

Someone cried out, 'Mildred? Mildred, what are you doing up there?'

A horse spirit approached from the lobby, moving eagerly up the stairs. She was clearly a spirit that liked humans, as she walked upright, wore an elaborate pink dress and glittered with jewellery. She blinked her long brown eyelashes as she reached the landing.

'Oh,' she said. 'You're a little short to be Mildred. Are you a friend of hers?'

Bethany backed away a few paces. She wasn't entirely sure how she should react to a horse in a dress but running away in fright was probably not the best idea. Her eyes searched the landing for some hint of Quinn, but she knew that he had left her on her own again. The horse spirit towered over her. She looked posh and important and slightly intimidating.

Bethany nodded her head.

'Well, you'll know all about me, I'm sure. You can call me the Duchess, if you wish.' She shook her long mane, neighed and stamped one of her hooves as way of introduction.

Bethany didn't know if she should curtsy, neigh or clop

one of her hoofed feet in response to the horse spirit. She found herself holding out her hand with the ticket she had been examining as if she was about to shake hands.

'Why, I say, where did you get *that* from?' the Duchess said in amazement. She stared at the card greedily. 'It's not just anyone who is given an invitation to the restaurant, you know.'

Bethany smiled meekly and shrugged her shoulders. At least, she knew what the card was for now.

'It really is a generous offer,' the horse spirit continued, misunderstanding why Bethany had held the card out to her. 'I mean, I'm flattered. I really am. Are you sure?'

Bethany shuffled nervously on the spot, not wanting to speak in her hee-hawing voice and not knowing how to explain to the horse spirit that she wasn't offering to take her.

'Well, that's decided then!' the Duchess exclaimed before Bethany could respond in any way. She hooked her hoofed arm through Bethany's and pulled her down the stairs. 'Any friend of Mildred's is a friend of mine. Have you been here long? It's like a dream, isn't it? They have a meadow on floor 91. I met some charming centaurs. Charming! I think I could stay here for ever, if the fancy took me.'

As she talked on, Bethany noticed a very slight, continuous tremor in the coiled strands of gold as if the hotel was on alert. Some of the ghost staff had noticed this too and were eyeing the walls nervously.

The Duchess talked on in a loud, excited voice. 'Did you see the lights go out before? It's put some of the other guests in a panic. Mildred, for one, doesn't like the dark. Of course, you'll know that anyway. So I asked one of the bellboys what had happened and do you know what he told me?'

Bethany shook her head distractedly. She couldn't help thinking that maybe having the Duchess with her might help her remain inconspicuous. After all, the horse spirit was radiant with light and it took the attention away from her own distinctly weaker glow.

'Leprechauns,' the Duchess explained. 'They were behind it. They're trying to ruin it for everyone. No wonder they have such a bad reputation.'

Bethany fought the impulse to say something. As they moved through the lobby, she saw Stoames and Graceson appearing by the front desk. Just behind them was the bear spirit she had bumped into. The ghost staff were being given instructions. By the way Stoames mimed someone with long ears and a tail, she could tell that she had been identified. She ducked into a doorway.

'I say, we're not going to the dance floor,' declared the Duchess, oblivious to the manhunt about to take place. She pulled Bethany out of the doorway and swung her round to face the restaurant entrance. 'Maybe later. There's a wood spirit I've had my eye on. Wonderful foliage. I distinctly remember him saying he would be here.'

As they stepped forward, a maître d' in a smart waiter's uniform appeared from behind a set of swing doors and gave them a brief, disdainful glance before smiling politely and saying, 'Sorry, ladies. But the restaurant is by invitation only, I'm afraid.'

'Of course,' the Duchess chuckled and budged Bethany forward. She timidly handed over the gold card to the ghost and he frowned at it disbelievingly, turning it over in his hand several times as if he expected to find some evidence that it was a fake.

'Yes, well, that *seems* to be in order,' he said eventually. He grinned insincerely and begrudgingly held open the door for Bethany and the Duchess. 'If you would like to follow me, please.'

CHAPTER FOURTEEN

A TASTE OF FREEDOM

The maître d' led them through the restaurant. It was an elegant, refined affair, separated into several dining areas with each section filled with spirits of different kinds. The perfectly white, round tables they sat at appeared to be flat-capped mushrooms that sprouted in relation to the size of the diners. There was a shambling pumpkin-head creature sitting with a gigantic rabbit at a wide table. At one particularly short table, a group of gnomes were hunched over menus.

It was just as unexpected a place as Bethany expected it to be. Unlike most restaurants, it was an incredibly quiet, sedate place. Especially since all the guests had their heads stuck firmly into their menus. Some of them had even resorted to licking the menus – there was no food to be seen on their tables.

The Duchess preened herself as they moved through the

restaurant. She seemed to expect many admiring glances with the way she glided gracefully past busy tables. She was soon disappointed, though, as she failed to turn a single head. The maître d' ushered them to an area off the main dining hall where a dozen or so tables were arranged in a semi-circle. Much to the Duchess's satisfaction they were placed beside a party of woodland spirits and she shook her mane in excitement.

'A special table for two very special guests,' the maître d' said, directing them to their seats. 'I do hope it is to your satisfaction.'

Mushroom seats sprouted from the floor as they took their places at the table, supporting their weight like spongy beanbags. The ghost passed each of them a menu and a black pencil. 'If there are any problems, do not hesitate to call me over.' He smacked his lips and grinned in a way that Bethany found slightly menacing. 'Enjoy!' he said.

'Thank you so much,' the Duchess blurted out and gave a brief whinny.

The maître d' bowed formally and returned the way he had come. As he glanced back at them, though, Bethany could see his expression become suspicious. She trembled and hid her face behind the menu, hoping that he wouldn't notice that she wasn't a real spirit. If the hotel staff were already looking for her, she needed to make sure she was as inconspicuous as possible and that meant blending in.

The Duchess cleared her throat. 'You first, my dear,' she said.

Bethany flinched. The calm atmosphere of the restaurant

was at complete odds with her nervous state. She wanted to be searching for the giant's tongue, not sitting here choosing food. She reluctantly turned her attention to the menu book and noticed that there must have been some mistake as she had been given one that was completely blank. She looked from the Duchess to her empty menu and felt a creeping dread. The last thing she wanted to do was call the maître d' back over in her braying voice.

'Maybe I should start,' the Duchess suggested tactfully, picking up on Bethany's agitation.

She placed her menu flat on the table. It was also blank but as she lifted a hoof the black pencil leaped into the air in response. She made a scribbling gesture and the pencil magically began writing on the menu. Bethany leaned in closely to watch as the pencil wrote out *Golden hay* on the empty page, then very carefully and precisely, the Duchess bent down and licked the page where she had written the words.

Bethany thought it best to copy her, even though it seemed she had gone completely mad. She scribbled *Golden hay* into her menu then dutifully licked the words. She coughed and retched at once, as her mouth was filled with the dry, grassy taste of hay. The Duchess frowned at her, trying to cover up the bad manners by talking in a loud voice.

'I quite agree. I've always favoured wild grass too. There's nothing to compare to running around woodland at the break of dawn and tasting that first glorious mouthful of wild grass.'

She was clearly hoping to be overheard by the wood

spirits and one of them turned its bushy head in her direction.

It took Bethany a while to stop gagging. She looked around for a glass of water and, failing to see anything even resembling water, wrote *Water* in the menu and licked it. It immediately felt like she had taken a deep, satisfying gulp of refreshing water. The disgusting taste of hay disappeared.

Now she understood why all the guests were sitting so quietly with their heads stuck in the menus. They were feasting. She couldn't resist quickly writing down her favourite food to test this magic: *Double chocolate ice cream.* As she lick-read the words she found herself tasting the best double chocolate ice cream in her life and she gave a loud murmur of satisfaction. This, she had to admit, was an impressive type of magic.

The Duchess laughed as if Bethany had said something funny. 'Well, of course I love the woods. What's not to love? If I had my way, I would do away with cities and return everything to woodland. Don't all spirits feel at home in the woods?'

Ignoring her, Bethany excitedly scribbled out a long sentence of flavours. *Vanilla raspberry cake fizzing foam banana bun surprise.* The tastes exploded on her tongue and she marvelled at the way each of the individual ingredients combined. 'This is brilliant!' she exclaimed.

The noise that actually came out of her mouth, though, was a loud braying wail and the Duchess looked away with acute embarrassment. A few of the wood spirits lifted their heads and Bethany sank in her chair, remembering that she was supposed to be looking for the giant's tongue, not enjoying herself. Time was running out. She put the menu down and scanned the room for staff.

When the coast was clear, she deliberately dropped her pencil on to the floor. As she bent down to pick it up she crawled along the ground, hiding herself behind the wood spirits. She briefly peeked at their menus as she sneaked past and noticed they were full of phrases such as, *Spring shower*, *Midsummer sunshine* and *Refreshing breeze*. She scuttled to the next table. From here, she had a clear view of the main dining area.

She scrutinised the scene of spirits huddled around the tables, all quietly lost in their own menus. Some of them were greedily slobbering away as they filled the pages with new taste sensations, while others seemed to have fallen into a sluggish stupor and could barely lift their heads. All of them, though, shared the same glazed, vacant expressions that instantly reminded Bethany of the hypnotised villagers and her own parents. They were all in various stages of the same consuming trance.

A pair of waiters approached a nearby table full of gnomes and Bethany had to duck to avoid being seen. One of the short spirits had slumped forwards in a state of exhaustion. He was thin and pale, not at all like the plump, colourful gnomes she had seen in the image vapour.

'Maybe a nice bath would refresh you, Sir,' one of the waiters said as they discreetly lifted him out of his seat. None of the others at the table noticed as the slumbering gnome was taken away, they were too preoccupied by their menus. The ghost waiters carried him through a set of double doors at the far end of the dining room and, for a brief moment, Bethany caught a glimpse of the hall of bathtubs that she had seen when she had followed Stoames. With a jolt of fear, she understood what was happening. This was where they were taking the guests from so that they could be drained of their energy.

She shuddered, thinking of all those spirits she had seen in the bathtubs, slowly fading away to nothing. But the shock of this discovery was immediately overshadowed by another. Bethany's eyes drifted across from the swing doors to the large golden sign sticking out of the far wall.

J's restaurant. A lick above the rest.

Below it was a gigantic golden tongue licking a menu.

She stared at it for several moments, unable to think or move. She couldn't believe what she was looking at and wasn't sure whether she should trust her instincts, but she felt sure that the golden tongue in front of her was exactly the right size to belong to a giant.

The pieces fell into place. Maggie-Maggie saying that it would be in a place of high magical activity. The way that everything the strands touched turned to gold so that a giant's tongue would have to be golden. And what better place to hide it than somewhere where the guests were so occupied they wouldn't even look twice at the walls?

She couldn't help standing up and staring at it. *It was the giant's tongue.* She was certain of it. 'I've found it!' she said in amazement, then realised too late that she had just made another conspicuous hee-hawing sound that disrupted several diners.

She turned to run back to her seat and nearly bumped into the maître d' who had managed to stealthily sneak up to her side. He raised an eyebrow. 'Is there a problem, Madam?' he asked.

Bethany stumbled backwards clumsily and shook her head.

The ghost's distrustful gaze pierced her. 'You seem to have wandered from your table, Madam,' he noted dryly.

She waved the pencil at him by way of explanation as if that was what she had just found, and she dashed back to the table. The Duchess was snuffling at the menu, lost in varieties of carrots, and had scarcely noticed Bethany's absence. She seemed to have given up trying to attract the attention of the wood spirits.

Bethany quickly scribbled out several flavours so as to appear normal. She tried *Roast chicken and buttered potatoes with gravy* and slurped it up. Then she wrote *Rhubarb crumble and custard*. Both were exquisite and gave her the sensation of enjoying a meal but without feeling remotely full afterwards. She glanced upwards and saw that the maître d' was still there, watching, and so smiled contentedly and wrote out another handful of dishes as if it was her only concern. *Friday night fish and chips. Raspberry jelly and cream.*

Her thoughts raced. Now she had found the giant's tongue she had to find a way of moving it. There was no way she could lift it on her own. She needed Quinn. Or the leprechauns. Or . . .

Out of the corner of her eye, she could see the maître d' hovering.

She jotted down a dozen more flavours. She had no choice but to keep writing and tasting them in the same way as the other spirits but it was making it hard for her to concentrate on a plan. Each flavour was infuriatingly delicious and she could sense the magic slowly but inevitably taking effect. It was as if every new food she tried made her a little hungrier and that craving made her want to try even more flavours.

Bethany had an idea. If she thought of things that could outfox the menu it might at least weaken the magic and buy her some time. She wrote *Unbelievable pizza* and found herself tasting a weird mix of clementines, fish and marshmallows. She followed it with *Endless liquorice* which was just that, then *November moon cheese* which had an impossible chalky cheddar taste.

Next, she deliberately misspelled words. She tried *Mishroom* and *Fishfungers* and *Strawbelly milkshake* and found the flavours subtly muddled. Then she tried something completely random and managed to come up with the single word *Turquoise* only to discover that, much to her surprise, the tangy, zesty flavour did make her think immediately of that colour. Finally, she thought she had tricked the menu by writing *Miaow*. She tasted nothing, but the subsequent burp came out of her mouth in a miaowing sound and had an unpleasant fishy aftertaste as if she had been eating catfood.

It was no good. The maître d' was still watching her from a distance as he talked to one of the waiters.

Bethany scribbled frantically, worried that Sir Stoames would be alerted to her presence before she could let Quinn know where the tongue was. She couldn't think of any other ways to trick the menu so wrote any flavour that came to mind. She recalled every sweet she had ever had, every flavour of crisps she had enjoyed, every type of ice cream she had tried. And as she did this, she was no longer doing it to appear like the other spirits so that the maître d' would ignore her, she was doing it because she was falling deeper into the trance.

Bethany couldn't stop herself. With each new taste she wrote down, another ten possibilities popped into her head, and her mind became jumbled. Momentarily, she forgot about the giant's tongue, about Maggie-Maggie and the leprechauns and Quinn. In her groggy state, all she could think about was an endless selection of food. She had burgers and puddings and smoothies and pastries. She had every combination of flavours imaginable.

The maître d' eventually wandered away, satisfied that she was no longer a problem. The hotel had cast its spell over her.

As her thoughts began to slip away, Bethany was dimly aware of something scurrying under the table, brushing passed her leg. It momentarily broke through her daze. A tiny, persistent gurgling sound came from the base of her chair and she glanced down. A rat with a quiff of pink hair was blinking its eyes at her very precisely. At the same moment the pencil in her hand scribbled violently across the page, possessed with a life of its own. It wrote out several words and the menu leaped out of her hand and convulsed across the table. Blue and orange sparks shot out from the quivering page, before it crumpled in on itself and let out a defeated splutter.

She gawped at it for a moment, confused, the vacant feeling lifting.

The rat sniggered. Slowly, its body transformed into the miniature Mr Quinn. He peered up at Bethany and clicked his fingers. Her long ears retracted back into her head and her face contorted back to its original shape. Her mouth could form words again.

'Oh,' she sighed, rubbing her head. 'Oh . . . that was . . . that was weird. I couldn't stop myself. I mean, it was like it wasn't even me.'

Quinn nodded sympathetically.

Bethany, gathering her wits about her, quickly checked that neither the maître d' nor any ghost waiters had noticed them. Fortunately, a large group of ice spirits had entered the restaurant and was keeping the staff distracted. She leaned down and whispered to Quinn. 'We've got to be quick. I've found the giant's tongue. It's here.'

She pointed through to the sign in the main dining hall and for once, Quinn's gurgling laughter stopped altogether as he was stunned into silence.

'You'll need to help me lift it. I don't know how but —'

Quinn was already looking down at his own tiny body. He snapped his fingers and began to inflate. In a few moments he was as large as he had been in the village, broad and strong, towering above Bethany.

'That's how,' she finished.

A chair sprouted out of the floor to accommodate his bulky size and he sat down as if he had just joined their table.

'Look, we need to work together,' Bethany told him quietly. 'We have to create a distraction, otherwise the golden strands will get us before we can even make it to the door, never mind the kitchen.'

They both looked at the golden threads spreading across the walls in every direction. After Donovan, it was clear that just a single thread was capable, if it so wished, of turning them into golden statues of themselves. But if there was one thing they were getting good at, it was causing complete and utter chaos.

'What did you write in the menu?' Bethany asked hopefully. 'That seemed to work well.'

Quinn shrugged his shoulders modestly. He picked up a napkin and wrote, *A taste of freedom.*

'Perfect. I'll write it down in as many menus as I can. It should cause enough of a distraction for you to grab the tongue. Okay?'

Quinn nodded his head and his quiff of pink hair bounced comically down over his beaming face.

'Just remember, we're going to have to move quickly as soon as you have it. The hotel will do anything to stop us. So, no mucking about. Right?'

He looked more serious this time as he nodded.

Without further ado, Bethany swiped the menu from the Duchess and wrote out the message, *A taste of freedom.*

The book exploded in bright green sparks and the Duchess whinnied with distress at being pulled out of her trance so suddenly. She could barely believe what was happening and seemed even more shocked that Bethany was no longer a donkey. 'Your ears . . .' she said with a vague note of dismay.

But Bethany rushed over to the table with the wood spirits, moving in a circle round them, grabbing each menu in turn and writing in it. They were all too shocked to do anything. A couple fell backwards off their chairs as their menus sprayed coloured flames at them.

A group of city spirits was next. They were unnaturally large and had surprisingly strong grips on their menus. One of them growled with a thunderous noise at the disruption. Bethany didn't have time to look back.

She ran from table to table, her unusual appearance giving her the element of surprise. She managed to make it through several groups of diners before the waiters noticed what was going on. Even when a ghost waiter did realise, he was too surprised by what he saw to raise the alarm. 'It's okay,' she explained to him as she destroyed another menu. 'Sir Stoames told me to do this. In fact, he insisted upon it.'

For a moment, he seemed to believe her. Then the maître d' appeared.

'You!' he wailed. His eyes widened in horror at her human appearance.

'I'm only trying to help,' Bethany said. He didn't seem to think so, though, as he lunged at her, shrieking loudly. She managed to duck past him and swipe another menu. She scribbled in it and threw it over her shoulder like a grenade. It crackled and exploded in his hands.

'Stop her!'

She jumped on to a table and scooped up as many menus as she could. Golden strands twisted and writhed across the walls as if they were in pain. Spirits rose out of their seats in groups. Their initial confusion turned to anger. Some were shouting at the staff. Some tried to catch Bethany. Others were walking out in disgust. Virtually every table smouldered with sabotaged menus. In the rising din and swirl of confusion, the walls, tables and chairs gave a brief flicker.

Bethany glanced over and saw Quinn standing by the sign, waiting to make his move. The maître d' grabbed at her and she fell backwards against a giant bumblebee that in turn knocked over a line of mud sprites. More spirits shouted in complaint and another series of flickers caused the restaurant to momentarily disappear. It was enough.

Quinn timed his moment with one of the flickers. His hand snatched at the giant tongue and wrenched it from the wall. His body seemed to swell and grow with the effort, as if he was summoning every scrap of magical energy. It came free with a deafening screech and he was sent rolling backwards.

Bethany ran over and tried to help him up. He heaved the giant tongue off the floor, quivering and straining like a champion weightlifter. He shifted it up on to his shoulder and gave Bethany a reassuring wink. It was strange seeing him this way, serious, strong and purposeful, without a hint of mischief or humour.

The lights flickered and tufts of golden strands twitched from the hole in the wall. In one of the flashes, the maître d' appeared, his face wide-eyed and terrified. Guests were shouting and screaming in an outraged rabble.

'RUN!' shouted Bethany.

CHAPTER FIFTEEN

BREAKING
THE SPELL

She led the way, weaving past the ghosts and spirits and finding a clear route to the exit. Quinn followed behind her, clutching the tongue tightly on to his shoulder and bounding forwards like a charging elephant. With his new imposing size he was happy to knock over anything in his way and Bethany found herself running as fast as she could, trying her best to avoid being flattened by him.

In no time, they made it back into the lobby where guests and ghosts were scattering in a panic. No one seemed sure what to do. The golden strands tightened across the walls, as if they were squeezing the dimensions of the hotel. The lobby looked smaller. Entire walls were becoming fuzzy and indistinct. A single thread of gold shot out in their direction and hit a passing monkey spirit, instantly turning it into a golden statue.

Quinn sprinted across the lobby towards the *Staff Only* door. Bethany hurried after him. Shadows streamed across the floor and down the wide stairway. They fluttered excitedly at the intrusion as the two of them leaped down the stairs and along the adjoining corridor. They rushed down the long hallway until they found themselves turning left and left again, caught in the endless corridor.

Several golden strands projected out from the walls like deadly tripwires. In unison, the pair jumped, ducked and dodged. Quinn knocked Bethany sideways through the nearest door as a coil of gold slashed through the air, narrowly missing them. She slammed the door shut behind them and they found themselves standing at the edge of a large, brightly lit room. Dozens of glaring lights were focused on rows of hospital beds. There were clothes rails full of costumes and cameras aimed at several ghosts dressed up in bandages. They had obviously interrupted something at a crucial moment.

Quinn and Bethany paused. They noticed the two distinct clocks hanging from the ceiling, one that had hands and numbers and seconds ticking away, and the other pointing to *Broadcasting* time.

They shared a look of mutual shock. It dawned on them what they had disrupted.

Two crab spirits were operating the cameras, whilst a tall, shrouded figure sat in a director's chair. The shrouded spirit shuffled a stack of masks between its hands and replaced the stern looking one it was wearing with one that showed an expression of sorrow. The ghost in bed followed

189

the stage direction and began to sob. There was the doctor Bethany recognised from the first episode she had seen, although now she could see a zip at the back of his head. He was in the middle of delivering his line to the patient.

'You see, we've had to remove some of your brain to stop the disease. Unfortunately, all your memories of your marriage to Dave are gone forever.'

The patient stopped sobbing. The performers momentarily hesitated as their attention strayed to the figures that had just appeared in the studio. A flash of gold shot across their faces. 'But . . .'

But that was the moment that everyone stopped and looked up at Bethany and Quinn. The actors might have been able to keep going through the intrusion had it not been for Bethany seizing her opportunity to take revenge. She ran directly towards the stage and Quinn followed her, his thundering approach making the television crew flee in a sudden panic. The director quickly found a mask showing a screaming face before he dived out of the path of the charging pooka. One of the cameras was obliterated as Quinn and the giant tongue collided with it. The crab that had been working it somersaulted in the air and landed on the hospital bed. His pincers slashed through the bandages of the ghost actress as he bounced off the mattress, revealing her transparent blue face. There were shocked gasps from the other actors.

'It's all lies!' Bethany screamed as she rushed on to the stage. She ran up to the doctor and pulled down the zip at the back of his head. His face began to crumple forwards as if it had rapidly melted under the bright lights, showing the ghost actor inside the costume. He managed to stop it falling off any further but was knocked flat by Quinn. The remaining actor screamed and ran away. In seconds, the entire set was demolished as Bethany led Quinn on a lap round the fake hospital ward. She finished by pushing her face into the lens of the remaining camera.

'Mum! Dad! You're being hypnotised. I'm trapped in the Stoames mansion. You have to help!'

A large pincer nipped at her hands, forcing her to let go of the camera. Several golden streamers fell from above and the crab about to attack her froze and turned a bright, metallic yellow. Quinn barged into her, his expression stern, and he motioned to the door urgently. She took his lead and ran, zigzagging to avoid any strands, until they had made it back to the doorway. Scenery, cameras and lights collapsed in a ruined pile behind them.

A single bluish light flickered from the row of houses on Stonebridge Road. Bethany's parents had just been about to go looking for their daughter after the episode of *What About Dave?* had finished the previous day, when the TV had switched on again of its own accord. The happy jingle announced another instalment of their favourite programme. It had seemed a little odd that it had come on again after such a short break and they knew they had something much more important to do, but even so they still found themselves sitting back down on the sofa and letting it wash away their worries.

That had been over twenty hours ago. As soon as one episode finished a fresh one began and the cycle of jingles, catchphrases and melodrama had melted away their power to think properly. Several times Mr and Mrs Chase realised something was very wrong and that they had to stir themselves into action. But whenever they tried to move away from the screen, the TV seemed to grow brighter and a very faint, very high pitched noise increased a notch, making them feel dizzy and confused. They would collapse back on to the sofa and let another episode of *What About Dave?* distract them before working up enough energy to resist again.

Of course, they had no idea that the broadcast originated from the Stoames mansion or that the mansion was a portal to the spirit realm or that some of those spirits were running around in a blind panic trying to generate enough magical power to keep them subdued. They certainly had no idea that the device that sent the television broadcast to their house also generated a hypnotic spell and that the vast array of ectoplasmic converters and amplifiers and valves involved in producing it were being pushed to their limit. Sparks and shudders issued from the device. The efficient blue glow began to flash a dangerous red. The team of ghosts and imps in charge of it looked at each other desperately, hoping one of them might have the answer.

The broadcast had never come up against such a resistance before. It didn't matter that the power kept increasing, the hypnotic effects could not make Mr and Mrs Chase forget their daughter or their love for her. Even though her parents could barely form a sensible thought between them, they knew that Bethany was in trouble and needed their help. With each effort they made to repel it they put the broadcast under even greater strain until, nearing breaking point, Bethany appeared on the TV screen. As she burst on to the set of *What About Dave?* it sent a jolt through both her parents and they leaped up from their seats at the same moment. 'BETHANY!' they shouted.

They watched in amazement as she ran around the fake hospital ward causing complete devastation. When she grabbed the camera and started shouting at them they could hardly believe what they were witnessing. 'I'm trapped in the Stoames mansion. You have to help,' she finished.

The TV crackled and went out as the broadcast finally stopped. Mr and Mrs Chase looked at each other with alarm as they tried to make sense of what was happening. It was like waking suddenly from a very strange nightmare, only to find yourself in another equally strange nightmare.

'But how did we . . .?' her father blurted.

'W-We've got to . . .' her mother stammered.

'I mean, it's not . . .'

'When did she . . .?'

'We're coming, Bethany,' they shouted at the blank screen. They ran for the door.

As the broadcast broke inside the hotel, it caused a slump in the power. A deep tremor rocked the foundations of the building. The network of golden strands fizzled and sparked across the walls in reaction to the broken magic.

Bethany and Quinn used the momentary lapse of

power to their advantage, sprinting up the corridor. In the mounting danger, Bethany found herself singing her favourite song. She didn't know why, but it must have helped her make a decision as she stopped at one of the many doorways and dashed through it.

She didn't recognise the storeroom at first, as it had been redecorated in a bright orange paint. Two sets of paint-brushes were at work on the walls. 'Maggie-Maggie!' Bethany exclaimed in amazement.

The twins scuttled down from the corner of the ceiling they were finishing off. Their faces lit up with joy. 'Well, there you are!' they sighed in relief. 'We were worried sick, dear. You running off like that. Anything could have happened. Who is your friend?'

'Oh, that's Qui—' But Bethany stopped and frowned at the sisters. They were staring interestedly at Mr Quinn, who was huffing and puffing under the weight of the giant's tongue. 'Maggie-Maggie, you've lost your glasses.'

'That's right, dear. It was when the lights went out on floor 303. Funny thing, really. They just fell off.'

'You mean, they're not stuck to your face any more?' Bethany asked in disbelief. If the glasses had broken free then maybe the hotel was losing its power over the guests.

'That's right,' said right-headed Maggie. 'And you know, it's the strangest thing. We can see perfectly clearly.'

'We can. And we've seen some very interesting things. This whole hotel. It's . . . well, there's something very strange going on.'

Quinn cleared his throat in a noise that signified that he

was charmed to meet the sisters but he was moments away from collapsing under the massive weight on his shoulder.

'We know all about that,' Bethany said to Maggie-Maggie. 'And we need your help to find the kitchen.' She glanced back at Quinn who made another noise, this one sounding like a goose being squashed under a double-decker bus. 'Quickly.'

The twins scuttled to the door. 'You should have said sooner, dear. All you need to know is the code.'

They ran out into the corridor and made for the nearest door. Their fists began to beat out the rhythm Stoames had originally used on the door to gain access. Quinn and Bethany eyed each other nervously. The series of slaps and knocks seemed to take forever. The corridor shook and rumbled around them. Strands gave a spasm across the walls.

The sisters beamed as the door clicked open. 'You see,' they said together. 'It's as easy as that.'

But there was a crackling sound and the sisters' smiles remained on their faces for longer than was normal. Their blue pallor took on a golden sheen and Bethany felt a wave of anguish.

'Maggie-Maggie!' she shouted in despair, but Quinn pushed her forward into the kitchens, away from the danger. They were too close now to be stopped.

A powerful, absolute determination seized them in the last run up to the pit. They sprinted past the flaming chef shrieking his orders, ignoring his screams for them to stop. They barged past a group of ghost chefs struggling with fresh ingredients for the pots, all of them shaking their heads and waving their arms in warning. A huge explosion of flames rose up from the pit. Toadeye and Longfoot looked up from the row of simmering pots and they shouted something urgent at Bethany, but she refused to listen. All she could think of was how much she wanted to destroy the hotel, how the magic of the golden strands had to be broken forever so that her parents and the leprechauns and Maggie-Maggie and the giant could be free.

She pushed on, overtaking Quinn, breaking through the last line of ghost chefs, dodging past Graceson as he tried to catch her. Her heart was racing as she neared the wide opening and caught a tantalising glimpse of the giant below. She felt a rush of victory. *They had done it! They had made it to the giant!*

She turned to watch Quinn take the last few paces to the pit but she was momentarily confused by what she saw, and even more shocked by what she heard. There was a terrible groaning wail, a deep and painful sound. Quinn had stopped short of the pit and was looking at her, horror-struck. He had dropped the giant's tongue and his hands clutched the side of his head.

Bethany felt strange. A vague, fuzzy sensation spread through her phantom body. There was a horrible moment of stillness in the kitchen as all eyes were focused on her. This time, it wasn't guilt she experienced, but an inexplicable sadness. She heard her own voice faintly, as if she was hearing it from the end of a long tunnel. 'Quick, Quinn. We're here.

Pick up the tongue. We've done it. Quinn?'

Everything moved slowly. She followed the appalled glances down at her phantom body. It was changing colour. She watched in disbelief as it turned a pale blue, spreading fast across her whole body, losing the strong inner glow of light. She had the unpleasant sensation of becoming suddenly cold, as if she had been plunged into ice water.

Sir Stoames stood on the other side of the pit. He was standing by her physical body that she had left in the cloakroom. It looked strange and striking here, every bit as weird as a ghost would appear in the normal world. Golden threads extended from the walls and were piercing it in sharp, stabbing motions. They seemed to be draining the energy out of it. Light disappeared up the strands like juice up a straw, until the body shrivelled and blackened.

Bethany looked down. She had become a ghost.

'It really is the last resort,' Sir Stoames said, his mouth curling upwards in a particularly spiteful sneer. 'Such a waste of a perfectly useful body; we could have used it in the cloak-room, but you really left us with no choice, did you?'

He turned away from Bethany to address the whole room. 'Well?' he said.

No one dared to meet his eye. Something sinister flickered in there. The nearest group of ghosts hurried back to work, emptying a pot of fossils into the giant's mouth. A blast of flames painted the room in a brief orange glow.

Bethany examined herself, unable to accept what was happening. She felt weak and insubstantial. She looked to Quinn for help but for once his grin had vanished. He made a sudden, impulsive attempt to pick the tongue back up and throw it in the pit, but several ghosts pushed him to the ground and wrestled the tongue free from his grip. His shadow pooled underneath him, holding him down.

She never thought Quinn had a face that could express guilt but that was the look he gave her now. His shoulders slumped, his lips quivered and he dolefully shook his head from side to side. They had been defeated.

'NO!' Bethany shouted. 'It doesn't have to be like this. Don't you see? You can be free. We just have to fight it together.'

Some of the ghosts hesitated. They looked at each other nervously. Even the head chef seemed to flicker indecisively. Toadeye, his face straining with emotion, took an impulsive step forward but Longfoot pulled him back. Stoames cleared his throat.

'There is someone that wants to meet you,' he said ominously. It caused any hint of disobedience to disappear and, one by one, the staff went back to their jobs. Graceson glanced briefly at Bethany, then looked away in shame. The ghost chefs she had worked with hung their heads. Only Toadeye met her glance and his eyes were rimmed with tears.

Her shadow appeared and marched her off to stand beside Quinn. Stoames led the procession out of the kitchen. Two of his ghost assistants tipped the statue of Maggie-Maggie and dragged it behind the several ghosts that were carrying the giant's tongue. They made the long journey round the endless corridor, carrying on and on in deathly silence until, at last, they arrived at the green door of Stoames's office.

CHAPTER SIXTEEN

INTO THE LAIR

They stepped into the forest clearing. The ghost assistants dropped the statue and the tongue and nervously backed out of the room. Saplings grew out of the floor to grab the abandoned objects and the feet of Stoames, Graceson, Quinn and Bethany.

They were pushed upwards on a platform of sprouting foliage. This time, though, as they broke through the tree-tops, they carried on upwards. It seemed as if they were about to be squashed against the golden ceiling of Stoames's office, but their heads broke through the surface as if it was water. It rippled and shifted about them in warm, fluid strokes, parting to let them through, then hardening beneath their feet to prevent any escape.

A long, wide room stretched ahead of them, bathed in a lustrous yellow light. It was so bright that it took each of them a while for their eyes to get accustomed to the intense glow. Overwhelming waves of heat engulfed them.

Bethany took a couple of steps forward, squinting her eyes. She could make out figures running towards her. But as she moved forward and her eyes adjusted, she saw that they were golden statues of terrified spirits caught in the act of fleeing this room. Her shadow shivered then nudged her along nervously, as if it sensed the danger also.

'They were all troublemakers too,' Stoames said, catching her anxious glances at the statues.

'I wasn't trying to cause trouble,' she replied.

'You weren't trying to cause trouble?' He sounded incredulous. 'Brought the kitchens to a standstill, destroyed the library, sabotaged the broadcast and damaged the restaurant, not to mention being caught in the act of stealing the giant's tongue. Which part of "causing trouble" do you not understand?'

'I was trying to help. You've been hypnotising my parents and everyone else in the village. And you've kept the giant trapped in that pit. And you've been tricking spirits and ghosts into working for you. I think you know more about trouble than I do.'

Stoames's face briefly darkened with anger. He tapped the ground with his cane and motioned for them to keep moving forward.

As the four of them advanced, Bethany noticed that the golden strands spread across the walls and ceiling, looking like thick bundles bundles of hair, so much hair that the room seemed to have been hollowed out from it. It spilled outwards in dense coils and whorls, pulsing with a burning, luminous energy that came from the powerful source up ahead.

'It's quite something, isn't it?' Stoames remarked, gesturing at the pulsing light. 'That's the energy that powers the hotel. Everything comes from here, every room, every hallway, every single illusion. This is the centre of it all.'

The whole interior filled with the sound of a deep, rhythmic breathing. Stoames cocked his head to one side as he listened to it appreciatively, then carried on, winding between the gilded spirits. There were ghosts, spectres and imps, all of them caught in defeated poses, and as he walked past them his smile turned to a nasty, gloating sneer.

'I know all about you,' Bethany said quietly, looking directly at him. 'You used to be his servant when you were still alive.'

For a moment, Stoames seemed genuinely surprised that she had somehow discovered the truth. 'Well, you have been busy, haven't you?' he said testily. He tweaked a nostril hair thoughtfully, then gave a curt nod of his head. 'Yes, I was his servant once. A long time ago. But now I am the one they all have to serve. When they can't pay their bills they have to come to me and plead and beg. Yes, each and every one of them, all doing exactly as I say because now I'm the one in charge.' His grin widened as he looked into the faces of the nearby statues. 'Look at me. I'm not like other ghosts. I'm not fading, I'm getting stronger.'

It was true. Compared to Graceson and now Bethany, Sir Stoames's phantom body shone with bright silver light.

'Is that why you do it?' Bethany said. 'Because he makes you stronger? Because he put one of those patches on your body so you can visit the real world? You're still *his* servant, though, aren't you?'

Stoames winced and broke out of his reverie. 'Now, little girl, there are things here you don't understand. Powers at work that are above you.'

She turned to face him. 'No. There are things you don't understand even though it's obvious what's going on. He's putting everyone into a trance. He does it in here to the spirits and out there to the villagers with that stupid programme.'

'They like the programme, though, don't they? Your parents. They've not even noticed their own daughter disappearing, that's how much they like it.'

'That's a lie!'

Graceson's head jerked up nervously and he started to say something. 'But they broke the broadc—'

Stoames silenced him by jabbing him with the cane. 'Even your stunt to destroy the programme won't make much of a difference,' he said to Bethany. 'We'll have it repaired in time for the next broadcast. We can even modify it so that none of the locals will ever remember anyone living at fifteen Stonebridge Road. As for your parents, well, maybe it would be good for them to join you. I mean, we can always use extra bodies for the cloakroom.'

Bethany felt her anger boil over. 'You —'

But it was Quinn who lunged at Stoames, his hands reaching out to throttle his neck. Stoames fell backwards, terrified, cowering behind Graceson as Quinn's shadow pulled him back under control.

'Don't, Quinn,' Bethany said, realising it would only make things worse.

Sir Stoames pulled himself upright and jabbed his finger at Quinn. 'I would be careful in here if I were you. This place is full of surprises.'

They moved deeper into the chamber. It was as hot as a furnace and as noisy, too. The long, drawn out breathing sounded like a gigantic set of bellows. Glittering pulses of energy shot up the strands with each shuddering breath. They originated from a gaping pit, flaring with coloured flames. Above the pit stood a large golden tree, its wide trunk divided into two main parts with hundreds of branches spreading out from them. The branches split into finer divisions, until they became the thick bundles of strands that made up the room around them. It gave the branching structure the appearance of a gigantic set of antlers, especially when Bethany caught sight of the figure sitting at the base of the tree.

Directly across from her, on the other side of the pit, was the spirit lord. He was slumped in a golden throne, his wasted body fused with the chair. His arms and legs were bedraggled and wiry and resembled the gnarly roots of a plant. His head was propped up in the chair and had been stretched and warped by the power growing out of it. His face was nearly unrecognisable, as it had been compressed under the massive weight of the branching antlers. Layers of wrinkles and folds made it look like he had been folded up with time, as if he had been asleep for hundreds of years. It was a shock after having seen the young lord in the image-vapour. This thing in front of her was monstrous.

'He looks so old,' Bethany said in amazement. She had expected him to remain young like Stoames. 'Did he never wake up?'

Stoames shot her a sideways glance. 'What do you mean?'

'After he was hit by the lightning?' she added.

He looked momentarily unsure what he should tell her. With a shrug, he decided it no longer mattered what she knew. 'Yes, he never woke up. This is the dream that has grown about him. This is what was created that day. And it grows stronger with each spirit it draws in.'

'This place, this whole place is his dream?'

Stoames held his arms open in a sweeping gesture that took in the entire hotel that grew outwards from this point. 'You can't help marvelling at it, can you? It's incredible, isn't it? It's like nothing that has ever been. A living dream.'

'You talk about it like it's a good thing,' Bethany said. 'It's a demon's dream. It's wrong. It's trapping all of us.'

He grunted. 'What would you know? You're nothing but a stupid little girl.'

'Maybe I am, but there are others here,' she replied. 'There's the giant and the leprechauns and the Duchess and all the spirits whose energy you're draining. None of them would think it's a good thing.'

'And there's me,' a voice said. Graceson let go of the giant's tongue that he had dutifully dragged into the chamber and he stepped forward. He pulled himself upright and didn't react with his customary series of stammering and nervous hand gestures as everyone looked at him. Even under the threatening glare of his boss he managed not to cower. In a very clear, precise voice, he said, 'I don't think it's a good thing.'

The silver blue of Stoames's ghost body glinted like the blade of a slashing dagger. He was fluid and quick and within a second he was standing over his servant, his cane arcing above his head, ready to strike. 'After all I've done for you!' he screeched.

Graceson fell to his knees and raised his arms to protect himself. Quinn dived forwards and managed to knock the cane from Stoames's hands. Stoames's eyes filled with hatred, the silver of his body glowing white.

Almost immediately, golden strands reacted and came wriggling to life. It was like the weave of a carpet undoing itself as the walls disentangled. Solid branches split apart into vibrating threads, hundreds and thousands of them collecting, extending forwards and focusing in on the intruders. The largest collection centred on Stoames. He quivered. His angry pose wilted.

'Sorry, Master. I didn't mean to disrupt you.'

The filaments of gold danced as they transmitted his voice. More of the threads gathered round Stoames's head. They weaved together, shaping themselves into a copy of his face. It was a freakish-looking thing, like the inside of a mask, as if he had pushed his head into the golden strands and left an impression of himself there. Each thread flexed and pulled to give it movement.

'Sorry, Master,' it echoed. The mimicry was exact, although it had a disturbing quality, having been summoned from metallic vocal cords. 'Master,' it said, mocking Stoames. 'I disrupt you. Sorry, I didn't mean to.'

Stoames gulped. 'Yes. I had to come. I finally have the ones who have been causing such chaos. The girl and the pooka they call Quinn. They have broken the rules. All the rules. And they've tried to destroy you.'

His own face sneered back at him. It had no eyes, since it was the one thing the strands couldn't capture the likeness of. This detail gave the mask a sinister quality, alive yet empty, and it made Bethany want to run away in fright, feeling that she was powerless against it now she had become a ghost. She stood firm, though, refusing to give in to the instinct to run.

'It's incredible, isn't it?' the mask said. 'They have been causing chaos, such chaos. Now they come. Only now.'

Stoames wrung his hands. 'It's taken time, Master. They have been cunning. They were involved with the leprechauns. It was very difficult to capture them. I'm sure you can appreciate it's not been easy.'

The golden strands above Bethany and Quinn formed into new masks. Bethany looked up at a golden, inverted version of her own face. It grinned a nasty grin, making her feel unpleasant, as if she was every bit as mean as the mask made her look. She tried turning away, but the flexing coils of gold made it hover in front of her no matter which way she turned. Quinn stood at her side, also trying to avoid his likeness yet compelled to look at it.

'Yes,' the three masks spoke simultaneously, using Stoames's voice. 'The leprechauns. It was very difficult to capture them. The girl and Quinn have done well.'

Bethany's mask swung down towards the floor. There, among the golden feet of dozens of frozen spirits, were several small statues. She felt her heart drop. Flannigan, Seamus and Pat were sneaking off with their pot of gold and had stopped to look over their shoulders as if they had just heard a noise. This was the pose they had been frozen in. Stoames's safe must have been well protected by the golden strands. Bethany felt sick with the realisation that she had helped the hotel capture her friends.

She turned away from the golden statues. The mask pushed in front of her, but she forced herself to step forward and focus on the slumped, sleeping figure of the blond-haired lord as a fresh wave of the coloured flames erupted from the pit.

'Why did you do that to them?' she asked.

The golden mask shaped an expression of surprise as it hovered over her. It was not used to being asked questions. 'Why?' It echoed the word in her own voice. For a moment it seemed unsure of how to react. Stoames sensed an uneasy shift in the strands and was about to intervene, when a dry, stuttering noise came from the masks. The noise resolved itself into an abrasive, inhuman laughter. 'Why?' it said again.

Bethany remained still as the golden reflection of her face loomed threateningly over her. She felt momentarily safe while she asked it questions. The voice deepened, changing from her own to one that sounded old and malicious. 'Do you know what it feels like to steal someone's soul? To take a spirit's life-force?' It sighed greedily. The sound made the entire room writhe unpleasantly.

'No,' Bethany replied steadily. She thought of the demon attached to the lord she had seen in the image vapour, the black flame that stole light. She felt as though it was trying to steal something from her now.

'Such pleasure! Such power!' the demon roared. 'You could not know what it is like to devour a ghost, or feast on a dryad, or drain the very essence of a spirit that thought it could destroy you.' It directed this last comment at Quinn, taunting him by forming the mask into a petrified version of his face. 'It's exquisite the moment they realise I have absorbed their power. All their hopes and plans gone for ever.'

'You kill them,' she said accusingly.

The convulsive imitation of laughter began again. 'No. Not death. Spirits cannot die. But they can be changed into something else. As one ghost fades its power is transferred to another ghost. Nature spirits diminish as city spirits prosper. The power of ancient gods becomes channelled by the new gods. I consume them and turn their power into my own. And I leave behind a trophy of them.' The mask motioned to the golden statues littering its lair. 'That is how I have made myself so strong.'

Bethany shifted uneasily where she stood. 'Is that what happened when you killed the stag?'

The face of the sleeping lord stirred with the memory of its origins. 'What would you know about that?' the voice hissed.

'I know that you were a man once,' she said. She thought of everything she had seen in the library. 'You were a man that made a demon stronger with your greed and I think that demon is in control now.'

'You dare speak to me in such a way, child? You think you understand what I am?' The golden mask rose above her as if preparing to strike, her mirrored face contorting into an expression of hatred.

'It's true, though, isn't it? It was the demon that made you kill the stag and it's the demon that makes you destroy other spirits. The demon controls all the magic in this hotel, the magic that keeps everyone trapped. And it's a demon that can never be satisfied. It's what you *are* because you can never have the one thing you crave.'

'Oh really?'

'Yes. You want to be a powerful spirit. But you're not.'

The golden masks were too astonished to answer. Silence fell on the room and Bethany and Quinn each looked up apprehensively at the branches above them. The mass of strands in front of Bethany tightened into a thick cord and lashed out, knocking several statues over.

'I AM THE LORD OF DREAMS!' it bellowed. 'I CONTROL ALL WHO COME BEFORE ME!'

'No, you try to control everyone by tricking them and scaring them, but you can't. Quinn and I resisted. So did the leprechauns. And probably all the spirits you've absorbed. Even Stoames tried to help me. He was going to let me leave when the next portal opened.'

'What?' the masks chorused as they all turned towards the startled figure of Stoames. 'Is this true?'

'No, I can explain . . . it's . . . well, she's lying. I just tried to . . . make sure . . . that . . . that —' His eyes filled with accusation as he glowered at her. A coil of gold launched at him and caught his cane as he managed to narrowly dodge the blow. It landed with a heavy clank by his feet. 'Master, please,' he cried in shock. 'I was only trying to make things better.'

'Master, please!' it mimicked him. Then in its own voice, 'You will be punished.'

'You see,' Bethany said. 'How can you be powerful if you can't even control your own servant?'

The wrinkled, exhausted face of the lord twitched with the slightest tremor. For a very brief moment it looked as if he was reacting to her words. A fresh wave of flames blasted from the pit and shimmered up the overhanging branches, giving the strands a revitalising surge. The masks turned in unison, no longer mimicking their individual faces but flowing together to shape the face of the demon. It was the young face of the sleeping lord but twisted into a monstrous mask of hatred and cruelty.

'And what would *you* know of true power, little girl?' it asked, closing in on her.

She stumbled back a few paces and nearly tripped over Graceson. 'I don't know about true power but I know what's important. Friendship and kindness are important.

Helping others is important. All the things you can't do.'

The thick bunches of golden strands that made up the mask flexed and swung back, preparing to strike. 'Then let us put that to the test and see who is stronger, shall we?' it said ominously.

The column flicked backwards and swung quickly forwards again like a cracked whip. She knew what was coming. As much as she wanted to scream, she would not give the golden strands the satisfaction of catching her in a terrified pose.

She thought of her parents, closed her eyes and waited for it all to be over.

CHAPTER SEVENTEEN

LAST CHANCES

There was a shove, a sudden force pushing her that she thought must have been the golden mask, except that the shove had come from behind her. She bounced on the floor, her shadow squirming about her. There was the electric crackling noise of the strands capturing a spirit, leaving behind a golden statue, but when Bethany opened her eyes, she still glowed blue. She looked up, confused, and could hardly believe what she saw.

Graceson had jumped forward to push her out of the way, just in time to take the full force of the blow. He had been halted in his heroic deed and turned into gold. Bethany was stunned. He had saved her.

The room shuddered in disgust and the golden mask seemed to weaken and wilt. It was almost as if the act of kindness had repelled its power and the strands moved in a sluggish, stunned fashion. Even the tree began to sway uneasily.

Stoames looked about in horror then ran over to the statue, screaming and shaking with fury. 'My best assistant! Ruined! Is there no end to the chaos you cause?'

But Bethany had been knocked to the edge of the pit and she wasn't paying attention to Stoames. She was looking down the long, wide funnel. It led down to another floor and it took her a few moments to recognise the kitchen from this angle. There was a brief glimpse of some chefs dropping fossils into the bottom of the dark chimney. And, as a fiery cloud issued from his mouth, she saw the far off giant at the bottom of the pit.

'Of course!'

Quinn pulled her away from the erupting chimney. They both shared a brief glance that moved over to the giant's tongue lying on the floor, then back to the pit. Stoames was rushing towards them while the golden strands were gathering strength back into the demonic mask and preparing for a second strike. Their shadows were anchoring them to the spot.

Bethany's eyes fell on another golden object. Flannigan, Seamus and Pat seemed to give her a brief twinkle of inspiration. Her hand rushed to the pocket of her spirit jeans and pulled out the tiny leprechaun bag. She emptied the contents into her hand and blew it into Stoames face.

'Yeartha don toory,' she said firmly, hoping she had remembered it right.

He inhaled the powder as he ran into the dust cloud. His

nose twitched and it momentarily stopped his fit of fury. His nostril hairs quivered as little sparks of light glittered around them. She had clearly spoken the spell that made things bigger as the tip of Stoames's nose rapidly enlarged. The nostril hairs must have absorbed most of the powder's effects as they grew so thick and long that they resembled large, black antennae. He screamed in disgust, then fell over as their increasing size overbalanced him. It made him look like an upturned cockroach as he struggled to get up.

'That's the final straw,' he said. 'You're in trouble now.'

But the threat sounded ridiculous and Quinn began to make the strange wheezing, hiccupping noise of his laughter. For once, he didn't attempt to subdue it. The infectious, crazy giggling burst out of him with such force that even the golden strands were affected by it.

'Don't you dare laugh, Quinn! This is the end of the road for you.' The oversized nostril hairs wobbled in the air comically.

This set Quinn off into a more giggles. He exploded with hysterics and the effect was as sudden and powerful as the laughing fit Bethany had caused on floor 303. The ground they stood on became soft and rubbery and began to bounce up and down, throwing dozens of golden objects into the air. Stoames's arms flapped desperately as he collided with the statue of his assistant.

'NO! SILENCE!' The golden mask dissolved at the outburst as entire branches split apart from the antlered tree. They seemed to be trying to absorb the laughter by conducting it along individual strands. Bethany saw why.

Whilst she twirled in a mid-air somersault, she caught a glimpse of the lord's squashed, wrinkled face beginning to form a faint smile. The golden strands circled round him, cocooning him in threads, doing all they could to subdue him.

'Quinn!' Bethany shouted through the machine-gunning sound of his laughter. 'The tongue.'

The giggling had weakened their shadows and Bethany dragged herself to the edge of the pit. Quinn, although caught in an uncontrollable fit of the giggles, managed to roll himself over to the giant's tongue. With one particularly powerful belly laugh, he caused it to spring up off the floor and land in his waiting hands.

'No you don't!' Stoames had caught sight of what was going on and used his massive nostril hairs to propel himself at Quinn. He screamed as he plunged through the air and landed on the pooka's belly. This caused Quinn's arms to jerk forward, which in turn made him launch the giant golden tongue toward Bethany. They all watched its path as it arced through the air.

Time slowed down. The tongue turned.

A coil of gold shot out from across the pit like a spray of water. Stoames's face pictured shock at what he had done, then disgust as Quinn embraced him in a tight hug. Finally, his features settled into a look of horrible realisation as the golden strands reached them. 'Oh no,' he said quietly.

The tongue whirled around and around.

Bethany looked at Quinn as he winked at her. The spreading gold claimed his grinning face. It seemed he had

had the last laugh as Stoames was caught forever as a statue hugging his one true enemy.

The tongue stopped turning as it connected with Bethany's head.

It dropped into her hands and she teetered on the edge of the pit. All the movement of the golden strands stopped. Stillness and silence fell on the entire hotel. She looked down into her hands, dazed, wondering what she was doing holding a giant golden tongue. She swayed, seemed to be about to regain her balance, then fell backwards, down into the long, dark chimney.

A column of gold shot after her with the force of a torpedo. It stretched and distorted as it followed her down, transforming into her own screaming face. 'Look below you, Bethany. Your plan is about to go up in flames.' It began cackling hysterically at her.

She turned as she fell, so that she was looking down at the giant's face. He seemed to be trying to focus on her. But she also saw the ghost chefs about to tip another load of food into the pit which would mean she would be burnt to a crisp before she reached him.

'Toadeye! Longfoot! It's me, don't do it!' she shouted.

The ghost chefs began tipping the pan. One of them looked up, though. Two bulbous, wet eyes glimpsed Bethany falling from the chimney above. Toadeye let out a shriek. 'Livinghands!'

Without any explanation to the other chefs, and fighting against his own uniform, he pushed the pan away from the pit. Hissing fossils scattered across the kitchen floor as angered chefs rose their voices in protest.

'Thank you,' she shouted at Toadeye as she hurtled past.

'Cooks stick together,' she heard him shout back.

'YOU ARE WORTHLESS!' screamed the golden mask.

The giant's face grew larger and larger, filling the tunnel like an approaching train. His features rose in recognition as Bethany plummeted to him. The tongue glowed in response to his proximity, the magical bonds that had been broken now attempting to reconnect. Faint wisps of light shot from the tongue's jagged seam, down the pit and into the giant's mouth.

The golden mask screeched like tearing metal. 'YOUR POWER IS NOTHING!'

The giant, having been saved from another mouthful of fossils, managed to generate a small charge of energy. He opened his mouth widely and sparks of light surged out to the tumbling tongue.

'YOU HAVE FAILED!'

The golden mask accelerated towards Bethany as she somersaulted in mid-air, growing a hand out of the speeding metal to snatch the tongue before it could land. The hand's aim would have been perfect, but Bethany chose that exact moment to kick her legs, pushing the tongue downwards out of reach whilst she sent herself hurtling in the direction of the giant's right cheek. 'LORD OF DREAMS!' she shouted at the mask. 'IT'S TIME TO WAKE UP!'

The tongue did not fall the remaining distance but was drawn inwards by hundreds of connecting bands of light, all glowing with the mysterious power that had been generating the hotel only moments before. The strands tightened like stitching and there was a brilliant burst of light as the two edges came together.

Bethany felt it all happen very quickly. She bounced from the giant's cheek towards his ear. She could see the golden mask now recoil in shock. The demon's face appeared instead of her own, angry and afraid.

Not only could she see the radiance flooding the giant's body and lighting up the entire pit, she could feel it coursing through him and spreading up into her ghost body. It filled her with a warm, nourishing sensation. She realised the significance of making him whole again. There was something huge and boundless about his spirit that made the air tingle with purpose.

An explosive noise accompanied the tongue's re-attachment. It was quickly followed by a rushing, inward sound, as if the giant was breathing in and sucking every single noise out of the hotel. Complaints from the lobby, gibbering from the library, cacophony from the kitchen, all rushed down his throat. Bethany felt her own screams disappearing as she held on to his earlobe for dear life. It was like being on the top of a volcano, feeling the first tremors of an eruption. He finished breathing in and his lips shaped a single word as the air rushed back out.

At the same moment, every single ghost, spirit and demon in the hotel found themselves involuntarily saying the exact same word, the word Bethany found herself saying: 'JACKOMUSS'.

CHAPTER EIGHTEEN

JACKOMUSS

'Jack!'

Deep in the core of Jackomuss a memory stirred.

'JACK!'

A voice.

'Oh, must you always daydream, boy?' The voice of his father, cutting through his thoughts as it always did.

Images formed, vague and fuzzy, disrupting the long forgotten past. The blond-haired lord and the demon remembered far, far back, back to the time before they had fused together, before they had hunted the stag. A time when the lord was a young boy and the demon was nothing more than a dark thought in his mind.

There was the castle as it had been in his childhood, sitting proudly at the centre of wild woodland. There were the busy kitchens where he would play with the cook's children amid the hustle and bustle of clattering pots and sizzling food. And there was the library, full of huge hand written volumes where he would read tales of terrifying wraiths and beautiful sea nymphs, reading them beneath the stained glass windows until the colours falling on the page seemed to fill his mind with wonderful possibilities.

Then there was the courtyard, the place Jack liked the least. This was where he had to practise his sword and archery skills with his older brother, watched over by the stone statues of snarling dogs that lined the entrance to the castle. There had been weeks of gruelling training with wooden swords and shields, guided by their father, a towering giant of a man who always shouted out his orders in gruff, demanding bursts. 'Get your sword higher! Lower that shield! Lunge!'

Invariably, Jack lost to his elder brother in these sparring sessions. Whereas Jack was of slight build and physically awkward, his brother Robert resembled their father – broad, strong and full of confidence. Day after day he effortlessly overpowered Jack and left him bruised and beaten, sometimes modest about his victory, sometimes gloating.

'Jack, you must try harder,' his father would chastise him after each defeat.

It was nothing unusual. Jack had grown used to the constant criticisms that would echo round the castle whenever his father found fault with him. At mealtimes: 'Jack, you must eat more. You have no meat on your bones.' When he played with the cook's children: 'Jack, you must not be familiar with the servants. You are their superior and must teach them so.' Or if he found Jack drawing one of his fantastical pictures of spirit realms: 'Oh Jack, you must stop with these fanciful notions. Sprites and spectres and such. How do you expect to have rank and power in the world if you fill your head with such nonsense?'

For each criticism Jack received, his brother was showered with an equal amount of praise. His father could not conceal his pride for his eldest son and would frequently tell him how he would one day make a fine lord and bring honour to the family name. He complimented Robert's sword skills, insisting he had never seen such natural talent before. He would regale his eldest son with tales of his own youth and the two would laugh together, a sound that deflated Jack.

Inevitably, Jack's resentment grew. His daydreams, once pleasant and full of innocence, took a dark turn and he began to let a voice intrude on his thoughts, a voice that answered the criticisms.

Look at them laughing, Jack. You'll show them one day . . . you'll show them how strong you are. Things would be different if you were the only son.

With each scathing remark from his father and each defeat from his brother, the voice grew stronger, and Jack felt its strange force building in him. Even though his brother consistently beat him in their sword fights Jack began to dodge attacks and occasionally trip his brother up. Several times he would keel over, faking an injury that made his brother look cruel and incur the wrath of their father.

This only aggravated Robert, who would enjoy mocking his brother's belief in ghosts and spirits.

It was on one such occasion, though, that Jack's cunning made him reply, 'They do exist and I can prove it. At dusk you can see the spirit lights out by the marshes at the edge of the forest. They're called Jack-o-lanterns and they lead travellers to their deaths.' It gave him a thrill saying his own named mixed with something mysterious and dangerous.

His brother laughed but he sounded uncertain and Jack seized on this.

'We don't have to go if you're scared,' he said.

'I'm not scared,' his elder brother replied, trying to sound indifferent.

'Well then . . .' Jack smiled. 'We can go tonight, but don't tell father. He doesn't like us playing out there.'

His brother tried to think of a plausible excuse for not going but reluctantly gave in. 'This better be good,' he warned.

An hour later they were trudging their way through the forest, winding past thick patches of crooked trees and across trickling streams. Outside of their father's influence Jack became confident and animated. He talked excitedly about imps that granted wishes and shape-shifting demons that would squeeze their victims to death and, of course, Jack-o-lanterns. 'They're also called will-o-the-wisps and they lure the foolish and gullible to their death. I prefer the name Jack-o-lanterns though. I think it makes them sound more noble. What do you think?'

His brother listened patiently at first, then begrudgingly,

until, eventually, he couldn't hide his contempt any longer. As they clambered over a mossy trunk he tutted at his younger brother. 'Sometimes I think father is right. You must stop filling your head with such nonsense.'

'It's not nonsense,' Jack replied. 'Anyway, it doesn't matter what I do, father has his favourite.'

The comment made Robert's cheeks flush with a mixture of anger and embarrassment. 'Father only criticises you because he wants to help you. You've heard him, you need to be strong to be a lord.'

Jack lowered himself down from the tree trunk and into the pooling darkness. 'I'll be strong in my own way one day.'

A chuckle escaped from his brother's throat. 'What? You? What will you be, master of ghosts? Maybe lord of dreams?'

'Don't laugh at me!' Jack said. He strode towards the edge of the woods, reaching a steep, muddy bank that over-looked the marshes.

His brother followed, managing to control his sniggering. As he joined Jack, the two looked over the gloomy, stagnant waters and Robert crossed his arms. 'So where are they, these Jack-o-lanterns of yours?' he asked, a condescending tone in his voice.

Jack looked up at his brother. He had planned to lead him out here and get him lost, but now that plan felt clumsy and foolish. 'They're up ahead,' he said. He marched forwards but his brother remained standing in the same position.

'They're not here, are they?' Robert sighed and shook his

head. 'Jack, you must stop believing in these things.'

'Don't say that!' Jack spat.

For a moment his brother was surprised at the force of Jack's reaction. Then it dawned on him what he had said. He stood tall, coughed, lowered his voice to the deep, gruff tone their father used and said, 'Jack, you must try harder. Jack, you must not slouch. Jack, you must be more like your brother.'

'SHUT UP!' Jack seethed with anger. He turned on his brother, face contorted by fury, hands bunched into fists.

His brother held up his hands in a peaceful gesture. 'Calm down. I was only joking,' he said quietly. He let the silence between them linger for a few moments before casually saying, 'Anyway, we might not have seen Jack-o-lanterns tonight but I think we caught sight of a Jack-o-must. Yes, a Jack-o-must-try-harder, a spirit that never quite gets it right.' He burst into laughter, loud and braying.

'I told you not to say that.' Jack felt his anger go wild. He felt the voice shouting out in his mind. *Show him. Show him what we are. Show him what we can do.*

'I don't know what you mean.' His brother shrugged his shoulders. He turned his back and prepared to return home.

The strange, rising force burst through Jack like a crashing tide. He finally gave in to the dark urges that had been tugging at his thoughts subconsciously for weeks. It was as if something determined and dangerous came alive in him at that moment, urging him on. He ran at his brother and leaped at him, aiming at a spot in his lower back.

'I only said Jack-o-muss . . .' But Jack knocked the breath out of his brother before he could finish the sentence, hitting him squarely in the back and knocking him down the steep bank. He tumbled head over heels and landed with a heavy splash into the marshy waters at the bottom. There was a sudden gasping, followed by the frantic splashing as his arms broke the surface, then a low, gurgling sound of something heavy disappearing into the muddy depths, leaving only a trail of bubbles behind it.

Jack felt giddy with vengeance. For once he had won and he didn't care how he had done it. In the gathering darkness, he watched and waited until all was quiet, then ran back through the woods. He felt this new power guiding him as he burst into the castle, screaming and breathless, telling his father of the terrible accident that had happened. He explained how his elder brother had taken him out to the marshes to prove that spirits didn't exist, only to trip over into the water in the dark. Jack's description of helping Robert was very convincing, telling an elaborate lie that he had pushed a log out to him so he could stay afloat whilst he got help.

The castle came alive as Jack's father involved every available person in the search for his missing son. A procession of servants hurried through the woods, carrying burning torches as they descended on the marshes. Their shouts and calls filled the night sky. Groups swarmed around the cavernous pools, dredging the water with long sticks then rushing on to another area. The atmosphere turned from urgent to increasingly desperate.

After hours of exhaustive searching, Jack turned to his father. 'I'm sorry. It was all my fault, father. I should have tried harder.'

For once his father appeared old. He did not look at his younger son with anger but held his shoulder reassuringly. 'No, Jack, you mustn't blame yourself,' he said quietly. 'You did what you could.'

The two of them watched the glowing lights hovering over the marshes, looking for all the world like the ominous spirits his brother refused to believe in and it took all of Jack's will-power to conceal his smile.

Jack-o-muss.

He transformed from that moment on. As his father mourned the loss of his eldest son, withdrawing to his room each day, Jack oversaw the running of the castle, commanding the maids and servants with an authoritative tone. Over the following weeks he became more focused, practising his archery skills with steely determination until he proved to be an expert shot. And he began to grow physically, developing an unusually strong appetite that helped him fill out his previously slight build. In almost every way, it seemed, he filled the place of his brother, even down to his appearance.

The months passed and no one could deny the dramatic changes affecting Jack, although few noticed the sly nature guiding him. When his anger flared and he humiliated a servant, it was put down to the pressure of losing his brother. When he encouraged his father to rest and let him take care of affairs, it was assumed that he was doing it out of kindness and not out of greed for further control. Nor did anyone questioned his sudden interest in hunting, or the savagery and frequency of his kills. In fact, so cunning was Jack's deception that many people felt sorry for him and thought that he had suffered terribly. They had no inkling of his true nature.

Jack-o-muss.

Rumours circulated after the second tragedy struck a year later. Jack had commissioned a commemorative statue to be made of his brother, sculpted by the finest artists and finished in gold. It was to be a surprise for his father on the anniversary of his son's death and so was brought in at night and placed on a plinth in the main hall. Something must have disturbed his father during the night, though, as he had woken and wandered from his room and, seeing the full moon shine off the golden statue in the darkness, believed he was seeing the phantom of his son hanging in the air. The shock struck him dead on the spot.

There was talk of a curse on the family. One of the servants claimed they had heard the dead brother's ghostly voice in the night, another thought that they had seen a figure wandering the hallway. No one suspected Jack, especially when he appeared so distraught at his father's funeral.

With the inheritance of land, wealth and title, Jack took on the air of authority expected of him. As he had assumed his brother's role, he now filled his father's position and his reputation as a formidable lord grew. If at times he came across as a little ruthless or greedy for power it was generally accepted that these were family traits. Gossip would spring up from time to time about his cruelty and that the tragedies that had befallen his family had unhinged him. There was certainly something off-putting in the way he treated people, the commanding presence that few dared to challenge or the way he could change the atmosphere when he entered a room. Stranger still were the occasions people looked above his shoulder at something they thought they had seen there, a passing impression of a dark and flickering shape.

All of which made Jack very pleased. He liked the feeling of power he had over others and he liked knowing that the source of that power would always remain a secret. He continually looked at the golden statue of his brother, admiring it as he would a trophy, and he commissioned one of his father to stand alongside it. He would enjoy seeing them together on their anniversary. This year he had organised a hunt in the woods and he had heard that an unusual-looking stag had been sighted. It would make a welcome addition to his conquests.

CHAPTER NINETEEN

THE
SPELLBOUND HOTEL

'*JACKOMUSS.*'

For a crucial moment, the power of Jackomuss faltered. The human and demon parts struggled with the memories of their origin. It was as if, in speaking their name, the giant had witnessed every thought and every deed that had given them their strength. All their secrets and lies were now revealed. The human part of Jackomuss reacted with the first stirrings of shame and guilt; the demon part of Jackomuss reacted with anger and fear at being exposed. One repelled the other and it sent a shockwave throughout the entire hotel.

Each illusion shuddered and went out. The branching network of golden strands appeared in place of every room and corridor and hall. They formed a shimmering maze consisting of hundreds of convoluted compartments spreading out in every direction. Each compartment contained the glowing points of light where spirits had been captured, and there were so many that it resembled a vast constellation of stars. For the first time the spirits looked about them and saw the hotel for what it was: an elaborate trap that had ensnared them.

Desperate and reeling, Jackomuss tried to control the situation. His form was spread too far and wide, though, and he had to shed huge areas of himself in order to conserve his energy. Parts of the hotel flickered back into life but the spirits were already rebelling in massive numbers. Worse, they were grouping together in order to resist him and his attacks. Whereas usually he picked them off one by one, the effort of taking entire crowds proved too much and it depleted him even further.

Spectres and phantoms gathered side by side. Sprites and ghouls rose up. Every type of spirit united in the effort to repel the golden strands. Having seen through the illusion that had separated them with their own greed, they now joined together to help each other break out of their prison. And the sudden shift was decisive. Jackomuss could hardly believe the speed with which his authority was slipping and his attempts at keeping hold of it became more hasty and desperate.

Golden strands began to wither and die. Entire patches fizzled away as the magic that they conducted dimmed and dwindled. Thick coils broke apart, branches collapsed. With each section, a part of the hotel crumpled, rooms and corridors shattering into pieces, carrying the chain reaction back to the mighty branched antlers of the sleeping lord.

Jackomuss woke.

In the chaos, the giant seized his opportunity. He shook himself free of his restraints and burst out of the pit. Bethany screamed and managed to grab hold of his ear. In two mighty heaves he pulled himself upwards, through the kitchen floor, disintegrating it, then propelling himself up from the rubble into Jackomuss's lair.

There was a terrifying shriek and Bethany peered down just in time to witness Jackomuss being destroyed. The demon must have realised its impending defeat and made its attempt to flee before the giant could catch it. Man and demon had been bonded so long, though, that their separation was agonising. The waking lord uttered a howl of pain as the black flame violently wrenched itself free from him and darted swiftly off into the wreckage of the hotel. The giant swiped at it once and missed.

The last of the lord's power collapsed in on him. A deluge of golden branches came crashing down as the antlers broke from his head. The coalesced stag and tree spirit that had made him so strong rose from the scattered ruins and returned back into their original separate forms. Although they were fainter than they had been, they were finally whole again and they drifted away. Even Jack's ghost was released as his remains crumbled to dust. But he was not whole like other ghosts. The demon had left a wound where it had torn itself away from him and he stared down in disbelief, the last of his light spilling out from him.

Jack screamed. He did not understand how any of this

had happened. His eyes searched for someone, anyone that could help him, but with a sinking dread he realised he was all alone and not a single spirit would come to his aid. As his essence sapped away he regressed back to a young boy and he caught sight of Bethany in his last shrinking moments, his expression pleading for mercy. He was not much older than she was now. She turned away, finding it too painful to hold his gaze.

The hotel came crashing down in an avalanche. Bethany clutched tightly to the giant as he made a series of motions with his hands and talked in a low, grumbling mutter of phrases. The illusions of the hotel were irrevocably broken but the fragments were still there and they began to fly through the air, orbiting him.

Yawning doors, leaping tables, jars of singing tongues and pans full of fossils whirled around in a chaotic cloud. It was like being at the centre of a tornado as hundreds of objects and spirits and ghosts rushed past. Uniforms of every sort danced and leaped in the air with shadows. The contents of rooms and suitcases mingled with the broken fragments of the kitchen and Stoames's office. Whatever the giant was saying made it all swirl round faster and that, in turn, seemed to gradually undo the magic as objects merged together then dissolved back into their original spirits.

Amongst the jumble, Bethany could see the golden blur of statues as they shot passed. With each lap they made round the giant, they shed a little more of their gold colour until they were transformed back to their original forms.

Spirits came awake and were set free. She watched keenly and saw Maggie-Maggie coming back to life. The sisters laughed as they held hands and spun round like ballroom dancers. They caught sight of Bethany, waved and waltzed off into the distance.

The leprechauns appeared next, hanging on in a chain to their pot of gold as it shot through the maelstrom. Donovan was at the end and smiled happily before they were finally carried off into freedom. Graceson followed, looking fearless and brave as he destroyed a cloud of flapping paperwork in a single swipe of his hand. He saluted Bethany as he disappeared.

Her heart skipped at the last bit of gold. Quinn and Sir Stoames circled passed. As the magic wore off them, Quinn looked around, confused at first then beaming with joy as it dawned on him that they had won. He found himself clutching the ghost of Sir Stoames, but it was no longer made up from authoritative silver light. Instead, it had a feeble, pale glow and Stoames looked appalled at his loss of status. He skittered away in fright from Quinn, disappearing in the direction of a smaller ghost he could order about. Quinn laughed and his pink quiff shook with delight.

Bethany couldn't help shouting over to him. His face lit up as he caught sight of her. Much to her surprise, he seemed to be trying to shout something back at her as his mouth began shaping words. She couldn't hear him over the whirling, thundering din. He repeated whatever it was he was trying to tell her, but she saw that he was shrinking, in preparation to disappear. She recognised the words 'you' and 'we' before he vanished altogether. Maybe it was another of his pranks. She waved farewell.

The next face she recognised was the most important – it was her own. Her body appeared in the litter of ghosts and hotel fragments. The giant must have noticed it too, as his immense hand reached out and he plucked it from the whirlpool of objects. He laid it out flat on his palm. It was dark and shrivelled and Bethany felt a renewed wave of shock that she was still a ghost. She could not return to the physical world. She would never see her parents again.

The giant carefully leaned down to it. Very gently, he blew on to the skin. It inflated and glittered with the strange light that had powered the hotel. He blew again, gently. Waited patiently, blew again. With each breath, colour returned to her physical body, then returned to her ghost body. She felt it in a warm flood of sensation, making her thoughts clear, bursting up through her in the most wonderful wave of excitement.

Maggie-Maggie had been right. The giant was a powerful spirit. He'd managed to bring Bethany's body back to life.

'Thank you! Thank you! Thank you!' she shouted down into his eardrum.

The giant used his other hand to pick her up from the side of his head and carefully lower her down to her body. A colossal expression of gratitude crossed his face as he nodded respectfully at her before he dropped her back into her body. The feeling was like being sucked down a plug-hole and she wasn't altogether sure that she liked it.

The last thing she saw amongst the swirling tower of

objects was the black flame. It had hidden itself inside a tumbling mirror and it emerged as the giant was momentarily distracted with Bethany. She shouted out to the giant as the demon flew away but her voice sounded too distant.

'Quick, he's getting away!' she tried to say. But the words came out jumbled.

She felt a moment of panic as her ghost body merged with the heavier, dense material of her physical body. The giant and the surrounding spirit realm became insubstantial. Her brain reminded her that these sorts of things couldn't exist and so her body decided that she must be dreaming. With that thought, she felt sleep wash over her, muddying everything she wanted to remember. She tried to fight it. She didn't want to forget. It was important.

The demon, she told herself.

Don't forget

It's important

The demon

Bethany

It's getting away

Bethany

'You've got to catch him,' she cried. Time telescoped away. Days or minutes could have passed. She was too groggy to know where she was or what was going on. She groaned wearily, looking around in a daze. She recognised the gates of the Stoames mansion and the bush that she had hidden behind but that had seemed so long ago it made her dizzy thinking about it.

'Bethany?' her father said in relief. He turned back to his wife. 'It's Bethany. She's over here. I've found her.'

His face appeared above her, pale and racked with worry. 'Are you okay?' he said. 'Does anything hurt?'

'I'm fine,' she murmured. He helped her sit up.

Her mother appeared, breathless from running, and Bethany couldn't remember having ever seen her so concerned in all her life. Tears welled up in her eyes. 'Bethany. Oh, Bethany. We were so worried,' she managed to say. She collected her daughter in a long, warm embrace and started crying with relief. 'Thank goodness you're okay. Thank goodness.'

'We didn't know where you were or what had happened,' her father said, sniffing. He struggled with the words, realised he didn't have to say anything, and hugged her tightly.

For a long time all they could do was hold each other. They cried and laughed, rocking back and forth, clutching each other tightly until it felt they had wrung all the emotion out of themselves.

'I'm sorry I ran off,' Bethany said eventually. 'I promise I won't ever do it again.'

'Don't be silly,' her mother replied, composing herself. 'You've got nothing to apologise for. We're the ones that . . . well . . .' The two adults shared a look of mutual shame.

'We've not been ourselves recently,' her father said soberly. 'I know that's no excuse but we've been bad parents. Ignoring you. Not spending time with you. It's no wonder you ran off.'

'*We're* sorry, Bethany,' her mother said. 'We won't be like that ever again. We promise.'

'But it wasn't your fault,' Bethany insisted. 'It was Jackomuss. And that TV programme. You were being hypnotised.' She looked around in the gathering twilight at the Stoames mansion for some evidence of what had happened but there was little to see.

'Yes, the, um, TV programme,' her father stammered. They had been trying their very hardest to put it out of their minds. 'Something very strange happened there . . . I mean, one minute we were about to go looking for you, the next we were . . . well, stuck in front of the TV . . .'

'And you seemed to appear in the middle of it all,' her mother added sheepishly.

'Yes,' her father said, sounding distinctly unconvinced by the explanation. 'Then we came up here. We tried to break through the gate but it was impossible. Even when I tried to get over the wall I kept falling back. It was like someone kept pushing me away. That's when we noticed the odd, glowing light. We thought we heard something so I tried the gate again but there you were, lying behind the bush. And that was . . . kind of strange, really, because I thought

I'd checked there already.'

He coughed and nervously scratched his head. 'It's probably stress,' he said weakly.

'No. No, it's not,' Bethany replied. 'It was the hotel. I got trapped there after I wandered in yesterday, but I had to wait until the portal opened again and so I had to work in the kitchens. But then I found there was a giant in a pit and Jackomuss had stolen his tongue so he couldn't say his name and me and Quinn went searching for it, which is how I found about . . .'

She noticed the uneasy way her parents were looking at her and stopped. She wanted to tell them everything, about feeding the giant fossils and cleaning rooms with Maggie-Maggie, and the things she had seen in the magical library. Most of all she wanted to explain about the strange and terrifying power that had been growing at the centre of their village for hundreds of years. But she couldn't find the words and she supposed that meant it was a story best saved for another time.

'Maybe it's not important what happened,' her mother said. 'Maybe it's just important that you're here and you're safe and that you know we love you very much.'

She kissed Bethany on the forehead. Without another word, the three of them stumbled home down the reassuringly boring main road, through the boring park, into their boring house. They were exhausted and confused but they were together and that meant they were happy.

CHAPTER TWENTY

HOME
AGAIN

Bethany sat in her room the entire next day. Whenever she heard a noise or noticed something moving outside, she jumped to her feet, expecting to see leprechauns scuttling across the floor, or furniture taking on a life of its own. She spent a whole hour watching her shadow, making sure that it followed her exact movements, occasionally spinning around suddenly to see if she could catch it off guard. It didn't help that her parents were checking on her every five minutes.

'Are you sure you're okay?' her mother asked for the hundredth time.

Bethany nodded. 'Yes. Of course. You?'

'Yes. Fine,' her mother replied in a strained voice. 'Everything's fine.'

Mr and Mrs Chase had started the morning by dumping their television unceremoniously in the bin outside and they kept peeking out the window at it as if they expected it to come on at any moment. They tried not to think about the soap opera or why they had watched it for so long or the lingering suspicion that their daughter had appeared on it. Even when they did think about it, they found themselves at a loss as to what exactly had happened in any of the programmes.

'Odd,' her father muttered. 'Very odd.'

They were similarly baffled as to why they had spent the last five weeks eating nothing but sausages. And why the local butcher's had now, for no obvious reason, closed down. Was there any significance in the garden gnomes lined up outside its front door?

'Beyond odd,' her father decided.

Bethany was having difficulty too. With each passing moment her memories were becoming confused and hazy. It was as if her brain was trying its hardest to make her forget all about her peculiar adventure.

It was after several days of brooding about these things that the mood eventually lightened in the Chase household. Bethany noticed the change in her parents. No longer dazed and preoccupied, they became attentive to her every need and never let her out of their sight for more than a few minutes. Her mother started to fuss over her, making all her favourite meals and showering her with treats that were normally reserved for special occasions. Her father compensated for his previously neglectful behaviour by returning home each night with a surprise present for her. Clothes, toys, books and games piled up in her room.

After a week of this, it became too much for Bethany and she stopped her father in his tracks as he offered her another parcel wrapped in shiny paper. 'Just a little something to let you know how much you mean to us,' he said.

She put the parcel down without opening it. 'Dad, you don't need to buy me presents to do that.'

'What?' He smiled nervously. 'You don't know what it is yet. It could be something really brilliant.'

Her mother appeared carrying a slice of cake and a fresh fruit smoothie, looking concerned. 'Is everything okay?' she asked.

'Look,' Bethany said. 'I know you both feel bad about what happened and you're trying to make up for it, but you don't need to keep giving me stuff.'

Her parents exchanged anxious glances. 'We just want you to be happy,' her mother said.

'Well, maybe we could just do more things together,' Bethany suggested.

Both considered this for a moment, then nodded their heads in agreement. 'Of course,' her father said eagerly. 'I was just about to say the same thing myself. You know, more family stuff. Maybe a walk in the countryside. Or . . . another thing.'

Her mother laughed. 'What, you were just thinking this minute how much you wanted to go for a walk in the country?'

'Yes,' he said, straightening up. 'What's wrong with that? There's nothing I enjoy more than a good walk.'

'If you say so.' Mrs Chase disappeared into the hall and

returned a few moments later with his jacket. She grinned. 'No time like the present, is there?'

'Oh, right. Yeah. Of course.' He begrudgingly put his coat on then gestured at his wife and daughter. 'Come on then, get a move on. I'm not suffering alone.'

They laughed, got ready, and followed him out the door.

The first thing Bethany noticed when they left the house was how busy the village seemed. It was as if everyone else had the same idea to get out of their house and enjoy the sunshine. The locals were behaving like normal people and it was very strange. Children ran up and down the street, causing mischief, whilst neighbours were exchanging gardening tips. The park was filled with fathers and sons organising a football match. Cyclists overtook a group of joggers who passed a line of ramblers. Bethany stared disbelievingly.

She was almost glad when their walk carried them out of the village and into nearby fields. None of them knew the area well, though, and it wasn't long before they were covered in mud and wondering which direction they should be going in. Her father led them across several fields until they ended up in one full of cows. The herd moved towards them and Bethany's dad hurried his wife and daughter over the fence.

'Come on, now. Haven't you seen humans before?' he joked to the approaching cows.

They looked back at him unimpressed and one of them broke into a loud moo that caused him to trip over the fence and land in a muddy pool. He cursed, then quickly picked himself up as if nothing had happened even though his coat and trousers were soaked.

Bethany's mother couldn't help laughing.

'Oh, that's right. Enjoy my misery,' Bethany's father said in a hurt voice.

'You were very brave,' she said, trying to keep a straight face.

He muttered to himself and walked on. They were now trudging through knee-high grass and Bethany was about to suggest they turn back, when her father made a surprised noise. 'What a strange-looking thing,' he said.

They turned a corner and there in front of them was the old stump of an oak tree sitting on top of a knoll. It made the hairs on the back of Bethany's neck stand up.

Her father decided to get a closer look at the stump, but as he strode up to it something caught his foot and he somersaulted in the air. There was a large ripping sound as a section of his trousers caught on a bramble bush and he landed in a messy pile on the ground. His head connected with the tree trunk and he groaned. For a few moments he lay on the ground very quietly, then let out a terrified shriek and jumped back on to his feet.

'Something just crawled over me,' he said, scanning the ground nervously.

'What was it?' Bethany's mother asked, stepping up on to a rock. 'It wasn't a rat, was it? You know how I feel about rats.'

'It looked a bit like a rat but . . . I think I must have really banged my head,' he replied.

'Why?'

'Well,' he rubbed his bruised forehead. 'It looked like it had pink hair.'

Bethany felt her heart beating quickly. She looked around in the deep grass. A gust of wind blew and the shushing noise it made as it passed through the grass was accompanied by the faint sound of laughter.

Movement twitched at the base of the tree. She ran over and parted some weeds. There, in the bark of the old, dead oak tree was a tiny message scrawled into the wood. She looked at it for a few moments.

We dream you. You dream us. Don't forget.

It made her shiver nervously. *Could it be . . .?*

Her mother and father shifted behind her. 'What is it? Is it a rat?'

Bethany was too lost in her thoughts to answer them. Everything she was trying to forget came rushing back to her. She recollected every detail of her adventure, including Quinn shouting something at her as he disappeared.

'We dream you. You dream us.'

She thought about it now, unsure exactly what it meant but thinking she briefly glimpsed its meaning, in the same way that she thought she suddenly understood Quinn's elusive nature. She laughed out loud.

Her parents became more concerned. 'Bethany?'

She looked over at them and moved away from the oak tree. 'It's okay. I think it's gone now,' she replied. She gave them a reassuring smile. 'Can we go back home?'

They nodded eagerly. The last thing her parents wanted was strangeness in any form. They practically ran back the way they came. When they reached the village they let out a collective sigh of relief.

'You know,' Mr Chase said. 'I think we should try a walk in the other direction next time.'

'Or maybe try a nature reserve,' Mrs Chase suggested.

'Or go for a day trip to the beach,' added Bethany.

They walked up the High Street, thinking of things they could do and places they could go. The sun cast the houses in a golden light. Some of the villagers were still in their gardens, even though a week ago they would have been rushing indoors to watch the TV. Bethany and her bedraggled parents stopped by the derelict butcher's shop and turned to look at the sky. They found themselves inadvertently staring at the Stoames mansion.

'How odd,' Bethany heard her mother say.

The building they looked at was nothing more than an unremarkable old ruin that no one had noticed before. Knowing that she would never again have the strange feeling that it was looking at her, Bethany smiled, and turned her back on it.